Indriði  18, 1926 first received attention on winning a short story contest in 1951 with Blástör, a humorous and erotic fertility story and a volume of short stories, Sæluvika. In 1955 he published his first novel, Cab 79. He was a prolific writer and journalist, producing several acclaimed novels, as well as poetry, short stories, biographies and much other work.

Indriði G. Thorsteinsson's son is the renowned Icelandic crimewriter Arnaldur Indriðason.

Williams & Whiting (Publishers)

15 Chestnut Grove, Hurstpierpoint,

West Sussex, BN6 9SS

Cab 79

79 af Stöðinni

Indriði G. Thorsteinsson

Translated by Quentin Bates

Williams & Whiting

A writer of his own time

Among the very first memories I have of my father is the rattle of his typewriter. A small office. Every wall filled with books. A mountain of butts in a huge ashtray. The blue smoke that enveloped him. And that urgent hammering, tap, tap, tap, fast, intense, driven to tell stories.

My father was never far from a typewriter and I knew he was a writer long before I knew what a writer was. Later on I came to understand that his best work was about the times he had lived through, and which were either gone or in the process of vanishing, and the changes that took place in Icelandic society in the years leading up to the Second World War and into his adult years.

He was deeply conscious of these changes and his first novel was about a young man from the country, like himself, who had come to the city and became a taxi driver, just as he had done. However, the city turned out to be a treacherous place and although the taxi driver of the story returned to the country, by then it was too late. It was was nothing but a mirage. My father called the book *79 af Stöðinni – Cab 79*.

He never returned to his rural roots except in his stories. He loved the city, a man who had been born in a dark turf farmhouse in a remote valley and laid on a foalskin. That was one of the stories he really liked to tell us.

By the time of my first memories of him at the beginning of the sixties, he was living in three-room apartment in a brand new block of flats in one of Reykjavík's new districts. Such was the speed of change, once the twentieth century caught up with us.

He influenced me as a writer; both his sparse style and the discipline of his working habits, as well as the stories he told of people losing their roots, bewildered and lost in the massive and fast changes taking place in society.

His old typewriter has a place on one of my shelves. Of course, it has long fallen silent. All the same, I can still hear the sound of it, the rapid tapping of the keys, as if the writer was in a hurry to capture the times he had lived in before they could fade into history.

Arnaldur Indriðason
Reykjavík, 2018

1

It was an evening in May and earlier that day four jets had flown over Reykjavík. They flew high and few people paid them any attention, accustomed by now to the whine of engines. The aircraft swept westwards over Faxaflói, passing low over the Reykjanes peninsula to land at the Keflavík air base.

It was a still evening. Three men entered the hotel and sat at the table by the palm tree. They ordered a round of doubles, knocked them back and asked for the same again. One of them was Lieutenant Martinez of the US Air Force. The others were his acquaintances, the little guy and the watchmaker, and they knew many of those present in the bar.

It had rained earlier and now there was mist in the air. There was a shine to the damp hair of those coming in to the hotel's lobby. The noise of traffic was muffled to a mutter by the mist, and the sound didn't reach as far as the group by the palm. The little guy lifted his glass. He worked in one of the ministries and back in the hard years his father had been a minister who had received little appreciation of his efforts.

With his glass held in his hand, he told Martinez that his name put him in mind of rum. Martinez liked the thought.

He was of Spanish descent, black-haired and stocky, swarthy, stub-nosed and with brown eyes.

1

There was a blueish sheen to his hair. He hadn't been aware that his name was such a remarkable one and he put a hand up to smooth back his hair, as black as a raven's wing. Long ago his forefathers had sailed across the sea following Columbus. They had also been called Martinez, and they had been just as stocky, black-haired and stub-nosed, with the same brown eyes. They had been glad to leave the old country behind, knowing that there was gold to be had in Columbus's New World. In whitewashed taverns where the hosts stood straight-backed under dim lights, they had listened to bearded men who had come from the west with talk of gold.

The ballroom had been brightly lit, but as the violin player lifted his bow, the lights were dimmed. A drum sounded and its beat continued, breaking into the the first number's regular rhythm. They clinked glasses and Martinez told them about Rosalind and the boy. He showed the little man and the watchmaker pictures, and they told him he had a beautiful wife and a fine lad. Then they raised their glasses to toast Rosalind Martinez in Denver, Colorado, and her son, Carlos Martinez.

A young woman at the bar waited to be shown to a table. Martinez gazed at her and she looked down at the counter, where her face was reflected in its surface, scarred with scratches left by knives and glasses. She looked steadily at the warped image of herself, seeing the dark shadows of her heavy lips.

His gaze went elsewhere, while she opened her compact, examined herself in the mirror in its lid and broadened her upper lip with lipstick. Martinez watched her follow the waiter between the tables, her step heavy, as if she were wading a stream. He had put his wife and son back in his wallet and Denver, Colorado vanished from his thoughts as he asked them to excuse him, getting quickly to his feet, clumsily, failing to push his chair back far enough as he did so.

They saw him lose his balance and take a tumble, landing flat on the floor and taking the palm with him on his way down. The waiters came over and righted the tree. Some earth had scattered on the floor. It was swept up and put back in the pot and dampened to help it settle. Martinez got to his feet, with earth on his front, in his hair and in one ear. The waiters dusted him down loosely with napkins, while he apologised to all three of them. He said he would be fine and they smiled in response. One of them accompanied him to the bathroom, brushing him down. He straightened his hair, scoured his ear and wet it thoroughly. Then he wiped his face and brushed his chest, long strokes and short, around the buttons, under the chin and across the shoulders. When he was done and had bowed, Martinez went back to the table. They ordered another round of doubles when he returned from the bathroom.

'How about a dance?' Martinez suggested.

They had already been drinking before they had gone to the hotel, and on top of that three doubles each had not made them any more sober.

'Make sure she's not tall, since you're so short,' the little man said. He enjoyed a joke.

'I don't care if she's short and fat, or long and thin. What man wouldn't want a woman after a year apart from his wife?' Martinez said.

He remembered their bed and the nights after Rosalind had come home after having the boy. The nightlight had stayed on and sometimes the boy wailed for her breast, and back then the boy had been the whole focus of her life. It wasn't until much later that he was allowed to touch her, when she had recovered and felt she could be intimate without discomfort. By now the boy would have grown and would move into his own room when he came home.

Martinez stood up, adjusted the knot of his tie and stubbed out his cigarette.

'We should have another drink before you go,' the little man said.

'All right,' Martinez agreed, and sat down again. His thoughts had moved on from his wife and child.

'You ought to leave the girls alone,' the little man said.

'We're not eunuchs,' Martinez said.

'It's a hell of a problem,' the little man said. He followed politics closely.

'Then here's to problems,' Martinez said and the little man felt that he ought to show more political understanding.

'It may well be that you've a talent in that direction, and that means you don't eat, haven't slept, you're awkward and cheerless, but all the same…'

'What?' Martinez said.

'The courtesy of small nations,' the watchmaker said.

'Time for a dance,' Martinez said.

They were both convinced that he had no shred of political awareness. Martinez stood up and raised his glass. His brown eyes were still and the light glinted on his black hair.

'Here's to the the courtesy of small nations,' he said. They smiled as he placed his glass on the table and left, passing a couple of tables before stopping. The girl turned away, pretending she hadn't seen his invitation to dance. He thought it had been by chance and tapped her shoulder. Their eyes met as she turned him down. He bowed to another two girls, but neither of them wanted to dance. Nowhere could he see the girl who had stood at the bar.

When he came back, they could see that he was hurt by the rejections, and avoided his eye. Then they clinked glasses again. He remembered how Sunday mornings had been when they climbed the hill behind the farm where there were rabbits galore. Old Jones's dogs had been fine hunters. Their excited barking woke him in the mornings. On the hill the dogs would be let off the leash to tear through the calm of the morning. The rabbits were easily alarmed and the toughest of dogs were the only ones that were any good for hunting.

'I reckon they turned me down because I'm in the army,' Martinez said.

'Who knows?' the watchmaker asked.

Martinez scowled.

'Bullshit,' Martinez said, still smarting at his rejection and the others were at a loss how to reply.

'They were a lot more friendly in Shanghai,' Martinez said. He grinned. The watchmaker shifted in his chair.

'Don't they have some strange clocks in Shanghai?'

They clinked glasses again.

'So, what were they like?' the small man asked.

'They were fine. It was a Japanese place and we'd been a long time at sea.'

'That must have been quite something after all that time?' the small man said.

'They powder themselves all over and you come out like a sack of flour.'

'You didn't see any clocks there?' the watchmaker said.

'Not that I remember.'

'The Chinese have some wonderful wall clocks. Their carving is excellent,' the watchmaker said.

6

'You're wrong, it's porcelain that they do so well,' the small man said.

'It's an ancient civilisation,' the watchmaker observed.

'Those whores powder themselves from top to toe,' Martinez said.

They ordered another round of doubles and by now it was late. Martinez had his elbow on the table and he was feeling fine. The others took to singing and he listened to them, right up until the doorman appeared and asked them to leave. The little man and the watchmaker stopped abruptly, halfway through their song. They shambled across to the statue in the square in front of the hotel and sat on one of the benches. The night wind blew off the sea and they said nothing, shrugging themselves deep into their overcoats.

Martinez was alone.

He looked up as a light slap caught his shoulder.

'Hey, there.'

'Hey, Sanchez.'

'What's new?' Sanchez asked, taking a seat.

'Nothing's new,' Martinez said.

'You better come with me,' Sanchez told him.

'You got some chicks?' Martinez asked.

'There's two girls at the table. Two's one too many,' Sanchez said.

'She's pretty?' Martinez said.

'Sure is.'

'How pretty?'

'Plenty.'

'Good,' Martinez said, and they went over to the table. He wasn't able to see the girls clearly. One of them laughed when she saw him, the one he guessed Sanchez intended for him.

'California, here I come,' he said, taking her in his arms.

The violin, piano and drums stopped playing. The bandleader placed his instrument in its case, took the flannel handkerchief from under his chin and laid it in there as well. The lights in the ballroom came on, but Martinez didn't let the girl go. He held on tight to her across the dance floor, through the lobby and out onto the pavement outside. They went across the square to the statue and sat on one of the benches. Martinez kissed her, but took no pleasure in it. He had no desire to talk to her either, and made his way onto the grass where he lay down. It wasn't her he was thinking of as he lay in the grass, and didn't notice who was walking along the street past him.

They had seen Martinez go outside with the girl, and watched as he walked away from her, as he lay in the grass and as she left him there. Now they went over, pulled him to his feet and helped him back onto the pavement.

'Rosalind,' Martinez said.

'What?' the watchmaker asked.

'Just you, Rosalind, and our little guy,' Martinez said.

'He's talking about his family in Denver,' the watchmaker said.

They walked towards to street, supporting Martinez between them. Now he was silent, saying not a word about Rosalind or the boy, but stood between them, shoulders squared, as they held him upright, while his head lolled forward onto his chest.

2

We were just starting a game of chess.

There was dance music on the radio and I glanced at the clock on the wall. It was just gone half-past eleven. We had already played a couple of times and neither of us had done badly. Guðmundur's knight was threatening my bishop.

'Cab Seventy-Nine,' the girl announced through the loudspeaker. There were only a few drivers in the waiting room.

'I can't lose work for chess,' I said.

'It's your move,' he said. The girl called my number again.

'Save your bishop,' he said.

There was a determination about Guðmundur when it came to chess and he wouldn't stop until the game was finished. He wished that others had the same dedication.

'To hell with the bishop,' I said and stood up. Guðmundur was stuffing tobacco into his pipe. He was around forty and a sharp chess player.

'Will you be back tonight?' he asked.

'No, I'll be going home,' I said from the doorway leading to the reception desk. 'I'll concede. So that's two games won and one drawn.'

Guðmundur lit his pipe.

'Let's keep track of the score,' he said quickly, knowing they would be waiting for me.

'Fair enough,' I said and let the door close behind me. I could see that the girl behind the reception window was impatient and the people I was supposed to be driving were outside on the pavement. There were lamps on the shelter over the doorway and at each corner of the building, and it shone brightly on the men waiting for me. There were two of them supporting a third man to keep on his feet. He was a soldier, his trousers sagging and his shirt adrift at the front where his tunic was open down to his belt. I went out to the car park and gestured for them to follow. The soldier staggered between his two companions and I waited by the open rear door, expecting them to get in as well. It was never pleasant having a blind drunk passenger. They made a respectable job of getting him into the car, his torso up against the seat and let him rest there, before manhandling one foot after the other onto the floor. It all went well enough and I held the door while they did what was needed. The lamp in the shelter shone through the quarterlight and onto one half of the soldier's face. His head lolled over the edge of the seat. His eyes were closed and the lower half of his nose and everything from there down was in shadow. But his forehead was bright in the lamplight, very clear and white-brown, the hair at the front glinting.

'Well, then,' said one of the men. He wasn't happy waiting, maybe more than he let on. Maybe he wasn't happy waiting as it was cold out by this time.

'We'll have to pay his fare,' the other man said, a hand in the breast pocket of his jacket. They had no intention of going with him.

'How much?'

'Where to?' I asked.

'Down south to the base.'

'A hundred and seventy-five,' I said. I could feel the chill of the night, and the darkness. It was uncomfortable having to take a man who was so drunk such a long way, and it wasn't even daylight.

'A hundred and seventy-five,' the other man said. He was a burly type, with grey hair sprouting from beneath his hat.

'I'll pay the hundred,' the first one said, slowly extracting a hand from his pocket. The banknote nestled in his hand and he waited a while with it like that.

'That's daylight robbery,' the grey-haired man said.

'There's no choice about it,' the other man said.

'It's still dear.'

'You pay the seventy-five. I have a hundred and it goes against the grain to throw it away.'

'I only have seventy,' the grey-haired man said.

'That'll do,' I said and pulled my coat closed around my neck. I'd had enough of waiting.

'If he wakes up, then try to get him to pay. Try and tell him he has to,' the grey-haired man said.

'If he wakes up I'll do what I can. But I don't think he will. He looks fast asleep to me.'

The grey-haired man dug a hand into his pocket and they both handed me their money. I straightened out the banknotes, counted them, took out my wallet and put the cash away. They both watched. Maybe they both regretted saying goodbye to their money, or they might have been thinking of what tomorrow would bring. In a few hours it would be here, in all its glory and without a hope of avoiding it. It would be a brand-new day, with white clouds and perhaps a coolness in the air. There would be women with bottles and pails up about early to fetch milk, straight out of bed and without any make-up and wearing Ulster overcoats that made their rear ends look unnaturally broad.

I got in, started the engine and gave it some gas. The engine covers rattled as I eased it back and I could hear the two of them as it ticked over. I closed the door and wound down the window.

'Before I forget, and just in case I can get him to pay, then I'm Ragnar Sigurðsson, cab seventy-nine,' I said through the open window. 'Just ask at reception for seventy-nine. I'll be in at midday.'

I put the car into gear, opening the throttle as I slipped the clutch. The car moved off slowly to begin with, very slowly, picked up and then made good speed. In the mirror I could see the glow of the lamplight from the roof play on the man's black quiff,

13

his forehead vanishing into the shadow and then hiding him entirely back there in the seat as I drove over the square and onto the main road. The traffic was heavy in town and it was slow going.

It was better once I was on the road to Hafnarfjörður. It was an uneventful trip and there was no traffic coming the other way. Every car was going in the same direction as we were. I had the radio on for ten minutes and heard *God Bless America* and the one about the flag with the stars before I switched it off. Before that they had played *Home on the Range* and *Sweet Heaven*, and I'd sung along with those. It was when we were coming up to Stapinn that the soldier started to mumble something.

'Hello,' I said, but he didn't wake up.

'Hi, there,' I tried, in English this time, but he didn't answer. So I recited *everything fell out as the barrel rolled* three times through. He seemed to have woken up by then.

'Rosalind,' he said, still more than half asleep. Then he was suddenly wide awake and silent.

'How's things?' I asked.

'Could I sit in the front?' he said.

I stopped the car. He got out and I opened the door for him. Once he had sat down and shut the door, I turned up the heater.

'Any smokes?' he said.

I handed him the packet from my shirt pocket and we each lit a cigarette.

14

'Damn this drinking,' he said, the cigarette held loosely between his fingers.

We drove south of Stapinn and turned in at the gate. They had lights at the checkpoint and beyond it the road had been covered with tarmac. The guards waved us through without stopping and we drove up the heath and up to the flight terminal. After a while he asked me to stop. The spring wind whistled over the cluster of buildings to our right.

'Is this it?' I said.

'Yeah. That's the Godforsaken place,' he said.

'All right, then.'

'Yes, this is fine. What do I owe you?'

'A hundred and seventy-five,' I said.

He handed me two hundred krónur notes that he took from a little black book in the right breast pocket of his tunic, which had the look of some kind of sports thing and was blue, as he was an airman. He adjusted his uniform and stuffed his shirt back into his trousers. I fumbled in my leather pouch for change.

'Keep it,' he said.

'Thanks.'

'Thank you, as well,' he said and got out, and slouched away between the sheds. It was blowing hard up there and the wind was in his face. I turned the car round, drove past the terminal and down the slope. At the gate two guards looked inside the car. They were faultlessly polite and as I drove off, one of

15

them lifted his hand to the brim of his hat in a salute. I did the same, except that I was hatless, but all the same, we were like chieftains exchanging greetings. The road outside the gate was deeply grooved, like driving across a washboard. This was a bad road for my old car. It was a nineteen-forty model that rattled a good bit but was otherwise in good shape. It didn't like the slopes and I placed a sympathetic hand on the dashboard. The metal was too cold and dead to be touched. There was a car on its way up Stapinn, but it soon disappeared, leaving nothing ahead but emptiness and the uneven road. I put my foot down, amusing myself trying to keep pace with the other car. All the same, by the time I reached Stapinn's top, it was nowhere to be seen. This one was a beast and there was nothing for it but to give it more gas. It was good to drive fast in the darkness, going hard into the corners and feeling the centrifugal force pulling the car back to the middle of the road on the way out of the bends.

I tried to catch sight of the car, but there were many curves and hills in the road that appeared in the lights, before disappearing back into the darkness behind. There was one more hill ahead. As I reached the crest, I saw a car stopped on the verge below. It was one of the post-war Buicks, more than likely the one I had followed from Stapinn. As I came alongside, I could see the hood was open.

'Anything wrong?' I called out of the open window.

There was no answer, so I got out and walked round to the Buick's front. The sidelights were on and in their dim light I could see a woman on her knees peering under the car. She must have heard me, but didn't look up.

'Broken down?' I said.

She looked round from under the engine.

'It boiled over,' she said, looking at me, but still on her knees. She put one hand on the bumper and got to her feet. It was an eight-cylinder engine, and I could feel the heat as I leaned over it. I checked over the radiator and couldn't see a leak anywhere, but the fan belt had failed and lay inside the fender. I reached for it and showed it to the woman.

'What's that?' she asked.

'That's the fan belt. It's snapped.'

'And what does it do, this... fan belt?'

'It turns the fan that feeds air to the radiator.'

The woman took the fan belt and looked at the ends.

'Can it be fixed?'

'No.'

'Can I get back to town without a belt?'

'I very much doubt it.'

'What'll happen?'

'It'll keep boiling over.'

'And if it does?'

'The engine will seize up,' I said.

'What do you mean by seize up?' Her voice was hoarse, and while she spoke slowly, the breakdown had upset her.

'It means a repair bill of a few thousand krónur,' I said, and didn't feel like describing to her what kind of a racket the engine would make, and how that would sound different to the hammering you get from loose gudgeon pins or tappets rattling. We stood in front of the Buick and she was almost as tall as I am. It was fresh and she looked down at the snapped belt. She looked to be around thirty, with dark hair and a good-looking face, but not beautiful. Maybe she was in the business and was coming back from driving her friend to the base. Or she could just as well have been in Keflavík. She had very fine skin, but her chin wasn't strong. She was dressed to flirt, in just a light raincoat over a flared dress, bare-headed and wearing red shoes with high heels. It must have been uncomfortable driving with those pillars under her feet.

'I think I might have a belt in my car,' I said, remembering that I had bought one a few days ago that I couldn't use. The woman looked at me and I could see well-shaped teeth. She had a heavy lower lip, and that made a few things cross my mind.

'You think so?' she said, relieved.

I went to my car, opened the compartment in the dashboard and felt for the belt that was there among

18

the cloths and rags. The woman had followed me and I held the belt up next to the snapped one.

'Looks like it might be too long,' I said.

'What do we do then?'

'Nothing, except that I have the honour of driving you to town, ma'am.'

She laughed. Maybe she felt I was being too formal.

'Or I can tow you,' I said.

'Me? No, thank you.'

'I mean your car, ma'am,' I said.

'Travellers in trouble together don't need to be so formal, do they?'

'No, my friend, they don't,' I said, and fetched a spanner from the compartment.

We went over to the Buick. When I had loosened the retaining bolts with the spanner, I pushed the dynamo up to the engine and slipped the belt onto the pulley on the shaft. After that I moved the dynamo back to tension the fan belt. It was slack, even with the dynamo as far as it would go, but even if the engine were to run hot, the radiator shouldn't boil up. I wiped my hands and closed the bonnet as the woman started the engine.

'To be on the safe side I'll stay behind you into town,' I said to her through the window.

'That's fine,' she said and put the car into gear.

'It'll run hot and you'll be best off driving fast. I hope it'll be all right.'

'Sure. And thank you so much for your help,' she said, emphasising her sincerity, her foot on the clutch. The faint glow from the dashboard was swallowed up by her dark hair. The shadows were deepening, rendering the woman's face both good and beautiful.

'We'll see,' I said.

She pulled away and was a long way ahead by the time I had got into the car and started the engine. She drove at seventy or eighty and my old car struggled to keep pace. She drove at a sensible speed through Hafnarfjörður, and then left me standing as soon as she reached the city tarmac.

3

I woke late and immediately remembered the money I owed the two men. There was no doubt that they would have turned up at the office to ask about it. It was around one o'clock, and I got up and shaved in my underwear. Maybe the woman had asked after me as well. There would be no end of ribbing if the boys were to find out about her. I hoped she wouldn't show her face, so they wouldn't have anything to play the fool over. These were tough characters and they stuck together, even though they made fun of each other. Some had nicknames that were never heard outside the office. If anyone were to speak with warmth and sincerity, then they'd turn shy. They had a deep suspicion of that kind of talk. It was important to them that nobody should get past their defences, to reach the warmth that they bore deep inside and which wasn't there for everyday display, although it was all the same a wholesome, true, strong and indelible warmth.

There was a good amount of cussing, filth and blasphemy, without any of it having much real meaning. These words stood alone and empty, and were part of their armour. Occasionally the old guys would explain sexual matters to the new recruits while they waited for a fare. Much of this was easier to remember than the first aid and other things that we were required to study for a licence to operate a passenger vehicle. There was more than just practical advice on engine maintenance, moonshining and venereal diseases that these old fellows had at their fingertips; they exaggerated, but were amiable and wry if the new boys didn't swallow their stories whole.

I dressed when I had shaved. The windows of the room were high and out of them I could see the roofs of houses in the spring weather. There were many red roofs, and further down were the tiled roofs of larger buildings with signs that were lit up. On the way down the stairs I met my landlady, who greeted me and said there was a letter for me. I went downstairs with her, took the letter and sat in the car to open and read it while the engine warmed up. The letter was from my father, with no bad news from home. He asked when I would be coming and said that the old lady would like me to write more often. I stuck the letter in my pocket and drove down the street.

There wasn't much space in the parking lot. When I had parked the car I went over to the canteen where we went sometimes to eat. Eiríkur and Róbert sat at the counter. I went to the toilet to wash my hands, and from there I could hear them joking with the waitress. She was a placid sort of girl who was used to their talk. On the other hand, the manageress didn't like it much when the customers joked with the staff. When things got loud, she'd put her head around the hatch and tell us to shut up. I heard the waitress ask what they wanted to eat. There wasn't a lot of choice, normally just a choice of fish, fried or boiled, or meat, fried or boiled. There was soup to go with it, milk, and coffee afterwards.

'I'll have the fish, soup and a glass of milk,' Róbert said. He was a mild sort and never rude to the girl.

'And you?' she said to Eiríkur.

'Fried shark,' Eiríkur said. 'And a glass of mare's milk, if you have it.'

The girl didn't answer. As I came back, she was in the kitchen. The manageress's face appeared at the hatch.

'You've a mouth on you, Eiríkur,' she said.

'And good day to you, light of my life,' he said.

The girl brought Róbert his soup and asked what I wanted.

'Soup, a glass of milk and coffee.'

'I'll have the fish and the soup,' Eiríkur said and the girl pretended not to hear him as she went back to the kitchen.

'Don't take it to heart,' Eiríkur called after her.

'You should know better than to act the fool,' the manageress told him, pleased that the girl hadn't answered him back.

'Wind your head back in, otherwise I'll have to come and sort you out,' Eiríkur said.

'And what's that supposed to mean?' the manageress asked.

'I don't discuss that kind of thing with ladies past childbearing.'

'Well, then,' the manageress said.

The waitress brought my soup and milk. I sat next to Eiríkur as he leaned forward over the counter towards her.

'I'd like to get you in the sack,' he said in a low, oily voice. 'And knock you up with quintuplets, sweetheart.'

'Don't talk filth to the girl,' the manageress said.

'What? There I was telling her what a fine lass she is,' Eiríkur said.

'I don't doubt you were being filthy.'

'Was I?' Eiríkur said. The girl wiped down the counter and didn't answer him and the manageress's face disappeared from the hatch.

'What do you want?' the girl asked, her anger gone.

'The fish and the soup,' Eiríkur said.

We finished our meal and went over to the rank. There was a crowd in the waiting room and I put my number on the board. Guðmundur was out on a call. I sat and read the papers. There wasn't much in them, no accidents, no house fires, not even a scandal, so it didn't take long to scan the news. The political coverage was deeply murky and the language overblown. There was plenty of treason, thieving and treachery in politics. The night drivers were showing up in the waiting room. Many of the night boys were young men who had recently bought their cars and put in the hours to cover their debts. Driving at night was a bad business, with all kinds of low-lifes and drunks about.

'Seventy-nine, there's a phone call for you,' the girl announced through the loudspeaker.

I stood up and went out to the reception desk.

'There's a Páll Jónasson asking for you,' she said, one hand over the microphone so what we said didn't reach the waiting room. She had the number in her hand and transferred the call while I went to the phone booth. I lifted the receiver from its cradle.

'Hello,' I said and heard the sound of a throat being cleared on the other end of the line. The door of the booth was open.

'Is that Ragnar Sigurðsson?' a voice asked.

'Yes.'

'This is Páll Jónasson.'

'Good day to you,' I said, unable to remember anyone called Páll Jónasson.

'I wanted to know if the soldier had paid his fare?'

'Yes, he did,' I said, realising that this had to be one of the two men from the night before.

'Ah. And he was all right?'

'He was absolutely fine.'

'Pleased to hear it.'

'I'll leave the money in an envelope and put your name on it. You can collect it from reception when it suits you.'

'Thank you kindly.'

'Don't mention it.'

I fetched an envelope from reception, put a hundred and seventy krónur in it and wrote on it; *To be collected. 170.00 krónur. Mr Páll Jónasson.*

I handed it to the girl and told her it would be collected. After that I went back to the waiting room and took another look through the papers. The weather was fine and there wasn't much work for us. Guðmundur drove past the rank and into a parking space. When he came in we set the chessboard up as it had been when we left it and I tried to think of a way of saving my bishop.

'Good trip last night?' Guðmundur said.

'Out to the airport at Keflavík.'

'You must have coined it getting a job like that to finish off.'

'It was a decent day yesterday.'

I advanced a rook's pawn to protect the bishop and while he considered his next move, I told him about the woman with the Buick, that I had loaned her a fan belt and she had left me in a cloud of dust on the road from Hafnarfjörður. Guðmundur made a bishop's move with his queen.

'You can write off that fan belt,' he said.

'More likely I'll lose this game.'

'You're going to lose the fan belt and the game,' he said.

'I have the feeling she's honest.'

'If she was out there on the Keflavík road in the middle of the night and in a new Buick, then don't expect her to lose any sleep over your fan belt.'

'What do you mean?'

'That's the way it is.'

'I don't see what you're driving at.'

'She'll have other business than your fan belt on her mind.'

'I don't care what else she has on her mind.'

'So this fan belt is of no importance to you?'

'The woman could be honest, even if she has other business to attend to.'

Numbers were being called up over the loudspeaker and I was getting near the front of the queue. It seemed that this game was going to be a tough one to finish.

'A hundred and twelve,' the loudspeaker announced. There was a pause. 'Whoever was driving a red nineteen-forty Dodge from Keflavík last night please come to the phone.'

'There's your fan belt,' Guðmundur said and I stood up to go to the reception desk.

'That's probably me being asked for,' I told the girl.

'Be quick,' she said, handing me the receiver. 'That's the rank's phone.'

'Was it you who lent me the belt?' was asked immediately, and I recognised that low, husky voice right away.

'Yes.'

'I lost you,' she said and the girl gestured for me to get off the line.

'You can drop it off at the rank. Just tell them it's for seventy-nine.'

'Couldn't you come and get it from me?'

'When?'

'This evening. It's the Faxen building, go up to the floor above the shop.'

'Fair enough,' I said, adding a goodbye and passing the receiver back to the girl through the gap in the glass. Then a man came in asking for a cab. I went back to the waiting room and took my place again at the chessboard.

'Was that the woman?' Guðmundur asked.

'Yes, and I reckon I'm not going to lose either my fan belt or the game.'

'The game's already lost,' he said.

The boys had heard the description of my car being called up. They came over and wanted to know the whole story, whether I'd run someone over or committed a robbery. I told them it was robbery, murder and moonshining, and Eiríkur told me to take a running jump.

'Ragnar's robbed some bloody Yank,' Hæi said. He was one of those who had been sentenced for taking part in the riots when Iceland joined NATO, and he had no fondness for the military.

28

'Seventy-nine,' the girl called through the loudspeaker.

'Let's just gloss over all that, shall we, dear boy?' Eiríkur said.

'I've already confessed it all,' I said from the doorway.

4

I went to see her late in the evening. There were lights in every window of the floor above the shop. I sat in the car for a while, letting the stress of driving fade away, and lit a cigarette. I realised afterwards that I had been on edge. I had been driving three men who had just arrived in town, certain that they'd get a result by driving along the main street looking for women to pick up. After I had been driving them for a while, I dropped them off at a dance hall and wished them better luck there. It occurred to me as I smoked my cigarette that I should have changed my trousers. Clothes weren't something that had been much of a concern for a while. In fact, there was little time for much other than maintaining the car, keeping an eye on its engine, its cogs and shafts.

The Buick stood at the entrance to the flat. The display lights in the window of the shop lit up the expensive fabrics draped over enamelled bars that had been artfully arranged behind the glass. These had to be wealthy people, and if she were a married woman, then her husband would offer me a glass of whisky. I'd have preferred a cognac, but this type had a fondness for whisky, certain that there was something aristocratic about it. Some brands were revolting and left people gloomy, taciturn and miserable. Her husband would genially talk business, of how difficult it was to get spare parts and what a struggle it was to get import permits for new cars. She would drop in the occasional affectionate word, then he'd fetch the fan belt, I'd thank him for it, and they'd again repeat their thanks. After that I'd be out in the street with the foul taste of whisky in my mouth, I'd drive for a while and that would be a good day.

At the same time, I was hoping there was no husband and that was an odd feeling. The steps up to the flat were covered in soft carpet with polished copper fasteners. I rang the bell and heard quick footsteps inside, and saw her appear through the frosted glass in the door.

She opened the door and said hello as she saw me. I said the same and she asked me in. It was the kind of greeting that I was sure meant that her husband wasn't at home, that he might be in England, or that he might be dead. It was too early in the year to go fishing salmon and nobody played golf at this time of year. She paused in the hall, as if she was expecting me to take off my coat. There were paintings by expensive artists on the walls. I wasn't wearing a coat, or for that matter overshoes or a hat. We sat in the living room and she offered me a cigarette. To begin with we sat in silence, very different to the night we had met out on the road.

'How are you?' she asked.

'Not bad,' I said.

'Are you busy?'

'It gets busy at weekends,' I said.

'The rabble needs to be driven here and there.'

'It doesn't matter who they are as long as they pay,' I said.

'Isn't it dreadful being a driver?'

'That depends.'

'And there are different sides to it, like everything else,' she said.

'Just like everything else,' I said.

'A good side and a bad.'

'And everything in between,' I said.

'Could I offer you a drink?'

'Yes, thanks,' I said. I almost said something different, but kept it to myself as it would have sounded awkward among the deep armchairs, the carpets and the paintings. It would have been particularly wrong to say it to this woman.

'Which do you prefer, whisky or akvavit?'

'I'd rather have whisky,' I said to humour her, and hoped it was a good brand. She left the room for a moment and returned with whisky glasses, soda and ice. She mixed my drink and asked how much, and I said I didn't want a lot, but she poured it half-full and it was a strong one. We raised our glasses and the ice hid the mustiness of the scotch.

'There's nobody to introduce us, and I have to ask, even though I know you're number seventy-nine,' she said, once we had sipped our drinks. She spoke quickly and seemed a little awkward.

'Ragnar Sigurðsson,' I said.

She said her name was Guðríður Faxen, and now I knew who she was. I said Guðríður was a fine Icelandic name, and a hint of a scowl appeared on her face.

'They call me Gógó,' she said. We sipped our whisky and I felt that Gógó was no kind of a name, but she was adamant that's what she wanted and we sat there and I called her Gógó.

'Cheers, Gógó. Fine whisky, Gógó,' I said. 'I'd gladly lend you a fan belt every night of the week.'

'It could have worked out badly and I appreciate your help,' she said.

'Don't mention it.'

'The car has been practically a wreck since my husband was taken ill. I haven't been taking proper care of it,' she said.

'Is your husband's condition serious?'

'Not very, I think.'

'Is he in hospital?'

'You're wickedly curious.'

'I'm sorry.'

'It doesn't matter,' she said.

Maybe I should have offered my sympathy for her husband's illness. But I didn't, sure that she would take it as impertinence. She stood up and went into the next room for something, returning with a photograph to show me.

'My husband, Ólafur Faxen,' she said.

He was a fair-haired man, tall and thin with a hooked nose. His eyes were close together, and there was an ugly scar that cut deep into the centre of his forehead. There was nothing special about his face other than the scar and there was a stiffness to him in the photograph, as if he was seeking a look of respectability that he was unable to achieve.

'He's in a mental institution in Denmark,' she said and I handed the picture back to her.

'It's that bad?'

'Yes,' she said.

'But they reckon they can cure him?'

'Yes.'

'That's an ugly scar,' I said.

'He was kicked by a horse.'

'It's the scar that's behind his illness?'

'Yes,' she said.

I looked down at my glass. It was empty. The ice cubes hadn't melted away, and rolled around the bottom of the glass. I could see them melting quickly.

'He'll have an operation. They say they need to remove cartilage behind the bone, where it healed after he was kicked.'

I didn't say anything. It seemed that this wasn't easy for her.

'More whisky?' she said.

'Yes,' I said. 'I'll fix it myself.'

But she didn't want me to. When she had refilled the glasses she sat down, her head tilted back against the chair. She sat and stared up into space, holding her glass between her slim white fingers.

'They're going to operate in the summer,' she said.

'Are you frightened?'

'You're full of questions, my devoted friend.'

'I'm sorry. But I'm not being nosy.'

'I'm not frightened.'

'That's good. Fear eats people alive.'

'As does solitude.'

'Yes. That as well.'

'This loneliness is making me a bad person. I'm completely alone. I've no children and my friends… Pah.'

'I can well believe it's unpleasant.'

She sat up straight in her chair and looked me in the eye.

'I doubt somehow that you understand,' she said.

'Maybe not everything.'

'No. Not everything.'

'Moral theory isn't enough.'

'What do you mean?'

'What I said. It isn't enough.'

By now I'd have gladly knocked back her akvavit as well. Later on she wanted to go for a drive and see what people were up to. I was in no condition to be behind the wheel, so we took the Buick to check out the crowds leaving the cinemas. I knew the rank and around the nightspots would be busy, and I saw

Guðmundur and Hæi outside the hotel. I hunkered down in the seat and they didn't see me as we drove past. Afterwards they'd be waiting outside the dance halls. I had the whisky bottle between my thighs and we had a drink in one of the side streets. Gógó was a fine driver. She cruised past the hotel again so I could see the guys waiting there while I was drinking whisky. They were driving for a few krónur, as now it was neither Saturday nor Sunday. There were no Americans in town this early in the week. Sometimes we'd have two trips to take them out to the air base on a Monday morning. If we could start at six and get back by seven-thirty, then there might be a trip with someone running late who needed to be down south before eight. It couldn't be done, but they'd offer a bonus if it could be done in half an hour, and they'd pay it even when the journey took forty minutes. That was because, if they could stand it, we had to go fast, with the car powering into the bends and coming out of them sideways, in no doubt that they were taking their lives in their hands. Even if they were deathly pale, their faces would go even whiter on the way and they'd slap your shoulder and say 'at-a-boy' at every trick pulled to earn that bonus.

We cruised until past midnight, by which time there were few people about, and we decided to call it a night. We weren't going to wait for the dance halls to empty.

'More whisky?' Gógó said. I said thanks and we
had another drink. She was sweet and pleasant, plus
she had a lovely figure and apart from that it was
good to talk to her.

'Are you married?' she asked.

'No.'

'Not even thinking about it?'

'No.'

'Maybe you've something against women?'

'Not at all,' I said.

'I thought men liked to talk about women.'

'Well…'

'They like to share tales of their experiences,' she
said.

'A man doesn't do that if there's any decency in
him.'

'You mean if the women are sufficiently
romantically inclined and in distress?'

'That's not enough.'

'What's enough?'

'Nothing's enough if a man's talk is genuine and
truthful.'

'If he wants people to think he's something
special,' she said.

'Exactly. I reckon their tongues are looser than
women's.'

'And their tongues are loose enough,' she said.

'On the other hand, women talk endlessly about
children.'

'That's another matter.'

'They aren't fully formed without a child.'

'Stop it,' she said.

'I wasn't going to say any more.'

'That's just as well,' she said.

'I was just explaining.'

'You don't need to. I know that none of us are what we should be without a child,' she said.

It was quiet outside and there was no traffic in the street. My head was empty, and that was the scotch's fault. I could never understand how some people could be so fond of whisky. Gógó stood up and went through the doorway hung with red curtains. She thought that men had loose tongues. Maybe she relied on them being able to keep their mouths shut. I caught a glimpse of the bed through the doorway as she went through. It was covered with a light brown bedspread with tasselled edges.

'Come to me,' she said from the other room. I went in and found it was a plain bedroom. She switched off the light and came over to me in the darkness, and turned her back to me. We stood there for a moment, and it felt strange. I didn't touch her, because I didn't want her to think that I was there for anything other than to collect that fan belt.

'Undress me,' she said.

It was what I had half-expected. Some women liked to steal the wind from your sails. I undid the buttons and slid the dress from her shoulders. She stepped out of it and I asked what she wanted me to do with it. She took the dress and laid it down somewhere in the darkness. I smoothed down the slip she wore, unclipped her bra and took the garter belt from around her waist. Her skin was wonderfully smooth and she placed the clothes somewhere in the darkness. She sat on the bed and I pulled off her stockings, leaving them on the floor. Maybe she was expecting me to undress. She slipped under the bedclothes and it was uncomfortable standing there in the darkness.

'Good night,' I said.

'Don't go,' she said.

'Why not?'

'Just because,' she said. 'Don't go.'

I thought of her husband in a sanatorium in Denmark, of the glasses on the table in the other room, the sour taste in my mouth of whisky and tobacco. My mouth was very dry.

'Sit with me,' she said, and I perched on the bed and looked at the strip of light that made its way past the curtains. I could hear the rustle of the bedclothes as she moved.

'Lie down,' she said.

'No,' I said.

'Please. Lie down for a little while,' she said.

I could feel the effects of the scotch. There was a wind blowing outside and spring was really on the way. I lay down next to her, on top of the bedclothes,

39

still wearing my shoes. Her face was close to mine and she laid one arm over me. I heard her breathing slow as she fell asleep. Once I thought it was safe to move her arm, I tried to lift it, disturbing her sleep. It was a while before I no longer heard the whistling of the wind outside and the light from beyond the curtain. Sleep came over me in slow, heavy waves, and although I tried to stay awake, I couldn't resist it.

5

I could see the grey concrete wall of the house across the street. The frames of its windows were painted red and my head hurt as I looked at them. It was morning and she was still sleeping, and had turned away from me. I gazed at the dark hair at the nape of her neck and on her cheek, and how her pale skin and the dark brown sweep of her hair met at her shoulders. There were no wrinkles around her neck and not a dimple to be seen, even though her head had skewed downwards in her sleep.

I breathed in the warmth of her and it was a delightful feeling, even though my head was sore and I still had my shoes on, lying on top of the bedclothes. I swung my feet off the bed and sat up. Sitting up on the edge of the bed gave me a pain behind my eyes. She turned over and stretched a hand out to the edge of the bed. It was white, as if nothing about her could be anything but white, and there was nothing glittering on her finger. Perhaps her husband had lain that side of the bed and woken in the morning with her hand draped over him, before he had gone wrong in the head and no longer woke up properly, no longer aware that she was by his side, feeling only the pain in his forehead.

The pain only intensified as I got to my feet; and getting to the canteen and having the waitress fix me a milkshake was all I wanted at that moment, and to knock it back without pausing for breath until the pain went away.

She was asleep when I left, her lips parted in a smile in her sleep, so maybe she was dreaming something sweet, untouched by the grey morning's hangover. It was too bright for comfort outside. All the same, I didn't want to bear a grudge against her scotch, because I had a liking for her, thinking warm thoughts of her as I started the engine and drove down to the rank. The waitress put plenty of ice in the milkshakes and I put away four glasses, thinking all the time of Gógó.

She was there instead of the heat behind my eyes, and she was there in place of the pounding in my head. She was blended with the milkshake that I was drinking early in the morning to dull the pain. Guðmundur came and sat with me, looking at me and the milkshake glasses. He looked old in the sharp morning light, and I felt a fondness for him, and for the waitress as I asked for a fifth glass. Guðmundur wanted coffee and my affection fluttered from the waitress to him and back to Gógó. The waitress disappeared into the kitchen, leaving us alone to drink milkshakes and coffee.

'It's that bad?' Guðmundur said.

'Not at all,' I said, grateful for the warmth of his friendship. It was a comfort and I wanted to tell him what had happened, how it had been, how I was feeling and how this woman was on my mind.

42

'So what were you drinking?' Guðmundur said.

'Whisky.'

'Ouch. Let's not mention that stuff,' he said.

'The whisky wasn't as bad as you think.'

'All the same, you've a hell of a hangover.'

'I didn't think it would show.'

'Your eyes are bloodshot,' he said.

'I'd best be off home.'

'Was she worth it?'

'It wasn't what you think.'

'Was it Kristín?'

'No.'

I poured some of his coffee into my glass, as the milkshake had given me a chill. It tasted foul and I thought I'd try a smoke with it. That was just as foul and I dropped it in the ashtray.

'Now we ought to take ourselves off and shoot a few geese,' Guðmundur said.

'You're out of your mind.'

'No.'

'We'll take a bottle with us and make a long day of it. And when we come back you'll have forgotten everything.'

'There's nothing to forget. It's just a hangover.'

'I know you.'

'You don't understand. I know how to be careful.'

'Then we'll take ourselves off for the day, since you're such a cautious type.'

'That's going to be uncomfortable, what with a sore head.'

'Another good reason to get away.'

'It'll be pure torture.'

'You're being soft.'

'Hell.'

'Come on, then.'

'If you really want to.'

'I really do want to,' he said.

We didn't talk anymore and he finished his coffee. We went from the canteen to his place to fetch his gun. It was a double-barrelled shotgun that he was deeply attached to and kept in a canvas bag. Then we drove to my place and I locked the car, as we were going in his. I went indoors and stuffed some cartons of shells into a bag along with a bottle of cognac. He waited outside. I took my rifle and carried it downstairs with the bag of shells. I wasn't a sportsman like Guðmundur and felt awkward letting myself be seen on the street with a weapon in my hands.

Guðmundur was a good hunter, and he wanted me to be one as well. We put the guns in the back and drove out of town. The whole day was ahead of us and Guðmundur drove slowly. There wasn't much talk and gradually my head and eyes felt better, so I didn't need to resort to the cognac bottle. I wanted to have a clear head in case we saw some geese, so it would be as well to stay away from the drink. We saw a couple of milk tankers coming the other way into town, but otherwise there was no traffic and Hvalfjörður was heavy going. By ten o'clock we were at Ferstikla and we could reckon on being in Borgarfjörður by midday.

'Aren't geese flying at this time of day?'

'I don't know,' Guðmundur said.

'At any rate, they're easily spooked in the afternoons.'

'Then we'll wait for evening when they settle down,' he said.

'You'll have to be pretty close with that Belgian blunderbuss of yours.'

'Talk about the weapon with respect.'

We drove through Leirársveit and the woman was in my mind the whole way. I tried to talk more about the birds. Guðmundur was helpful. He knew a lot about birds, and was happy to talk about them.

'They're very noble animals,' he said.

'Not the birds of prey.'

'Most of the others, though.'

'The ones that arrive in the spring.'

'That's the ones. All of a sudden they're here,' he said.

'As if they arrive by night,' I said.

'The calendar can tell you it's spring and the frost can fade out of the ground, but the truth of it is that you don't believe it until they turn up.'

'Noble birds.'

45

'Their arrival is about the only thing that won't let you down.'

'As far as the seasons are concerned.'

'In everything.'

'All the same, May isn't the usual month for them.'

'No, not at all. This is the month for change, turmoil and thaw,' he said, and continued his description of the month of May. 'There are still pools on the pastures if the snow thaws late in the year. Poems have been written about the brightness and the tranquillity and the plover's song like in no other place because spring arrives nowhere as it does here. There's a joy in being a child experiencing its arrival, and you'll remember that, because spring is no longer the stillness in the farmyard that we knew back home, and now we get the city springtime instead. And the next generation will no longer have a spring or the tranquillity or the sight of pale blue clouds over the mountains; and the springtime we know will never come to life again except in memories and verses about the stillness and the love for the land beneath the snow. Spring won't be found in a car, but instead in the cold meltwater surging around the feet of a child splashing through the pools on the pasture, and in its smell and its brightness and its earth. That's May.'

'You don't sound like a man on his way to kill some geese,' I said.

'Sometimes it can be necessary to shoot a bird.'

'Really?'

'Sometimes you have to kill something that's good, something you've a fondness for, to give cruelty an edge.'

'How so?'

'Either you're the hunter or you're the bird. If you're the bird, you have the nobility, but that doesn't help when you're on the wrong end of the barrel of a gun. If you're the hunter, you get to live. It's worth reminding yourself of that now and again.'

'You mean that applies in every sense?'

'Yes. Except now it's imperative to get you into the countryside so you can feel the spring and what it's like in Borgarfjörður,' he said.

'I know well that Borgarfjörður is a fine place to be.'

'Let's not get sentimental,' he said.

'Just as that's what I felt like doing.'

'That's because of the woman,' he said.

'No, it's because you were talking about springtime. In my childhood they arrived like yours did in Borgarfjörður, except that these were Skagafjörður springtimes and they always started with pools on the pastures.'

We were at the foot of Hafnarfjall and Guðmundur drove fast in the sunshine. The sea was a deep blue and slightly ruffled, but with a smooth white strip at the shoreline, sheltered from the offshore wind.

'It's good to see the country boy in you coming out,' Guðmundur said.

'That was a long time ago…'

'All the same, those country roots are there in me, in you and many others.'

'There's no need to let the roots die,' I said.

'No,' Guðmundur said. 'Not while there's some of its renewal kept in the places people live, in their energy and fertility and in the flaw in their pride.'

'And if it dies?'

'Then nobody will understand the first thing about this country,' he said.

We fell silent, as if there was nothing more to be said for the moment. The river was in flood at Hvítá, white like its name. We saw a few cars coming the other way and there were others ahead of us on the way to Borgarnes or up into Borgarfjörður. Maybe some of them were headed over the heath to the north. Guðmundur wanted to go to Borgarnes. He had a cousin there and suggested that we eat with him, which we did. The cousin was a pleasant man and Guðmundur gave him a bottle of akvavit. We opened it once we had eaten and had some in our coffee. The talk turned to geese and the cousin said that most landowners didn't allow hunting. If that were the case, then we could only shoot on common land, which Guðmundur's cousin confirmed. He poured himself a drop more akvavit, bemoaning the fact that he owned no land and that he had moved to Borgarnes from a farm where the marshes were thick with geese. By the time he had poured a few more shots, the land he had left behind was positively alive with geese.

He told us to talk to the new farmer, and as Guðmundur knew the man slightly and the lie of the land well enough, he reckoned that would turn out for the best considering the marshes were teeming with geese within easy reach.

We drove up that way and it was getting late in the day by the time we found the farmer. He said we could shoot in the marshes, and added that he was happy to have visitors. He was very amenable and came with us to see how we got on. We had to walk quite a way to reach the marshes and chatted all the way, although we didn't hear much of what he had to say as we were intent on the birds.

'Are there any ditches?' I said.

'No,' he said, and we went over the moorland above the pasture, skirting the bank so that we could approach it from below without scaring anything off. There was a broad expanse of marsh ahead of us, flat and featureless, and far from teeming with birds.

'No geese at this time of day,' I said.

'Be an optimist,' Guðmundur said. The farmer looked to see if there were any birds to be seen. He was the first one to see the group. They were some way off, and there was no way to get close to them as that would mean creeping down there from the bank. They could fly off before they would be in range.

'There's no hope of getting close to them like that,' Guðmundur said.

'Should I lend you a horse?' the farmer said.

'So we can chase them on horseback?' I said and we all laughed.

'You have the horse to hide behind,' the farmer said. 'They aren't frightened of animals and there are horses and sheep all around them. I have a horse at home you could use.'

'Then we'd need two horses,' I said.

'I only have one,' the farmer said.

'A sheepskin would do it, if you have one,' Guðmundur said.

'And who's going to wear it?' I said.

'You are,' Guðmundur said.

'I can let you have a fleece,' the farmer said.

'You're going to a lot of trouble,' I said.

'Not at all,' he said, setting off south along the bank to fetch the horse and the fleece. We sat and waited for him to return.

There was bright sunshine over the bay and in the distance we could see low brown ridges with mountains behind them that were practically midnight blue in the spring air, capped with snow-white peaks.

'There are further to the south,' I said, and pointed out over the marsh to where there were at least four

50

birds. These were closer to us than the others, and we'd have to pass by them if we were to get a shot at the larger group with the shotgun.

'They'll fly off from all over the marsh the moment we start shooting, even if we can't see them from here,' Guðmundur said.

The farmer, Sigurður, returned after a while with the horse and a fleece on its back. It was a reddish one, which was better than white. Guðmundur took the horse down to the marsh. It handled easily and willingly did as it was told. I pulled the fleece over my shoulders and made my way with my back hunched down the bank in their path.

'I'll wait for you,' Sigurður said.

There was a strong smell of sheep about the fleece and we were a long time creeping across the marsh. I followed a route to one side of them, and the ground looked wet enough to have ruled out crawling. As we approached the closer group, they lifted their heads to see, but didn't honk. So we knew this was just curiosity and not fright. Getting past the first group went well and Guðmundur brought the horse to a halt and turned it around so that he could see the other group from behind its head. The horse stood still and I moved closer. It was baking hot under the fleece. By now my birds were behind and within a decent range.

'We'll have to shoot at the same moment,' Guðmundur whispered along the horse's flank.

'You give the word,' I said.

'I'll say go, and then you can fire.'

'That's fine,' I said.

We slowly raised the barrels of our weapons. The movement alarmed the birds and they started to honk. I had the closest one in my sights right away and didn't wait for them to line up. They flapped their wings and the birds were restless as I drew a bead on them from under the fleece, waiting for the word to fire, but it didn't come. It was painful waiting for the word. The whole flock could fly away, waiting for it to come, unbearable and late... Then he gave the word in a low voice, and pulled the trigger with one report after the other, so close that they could not be told apart, and the narrow whine of the rifle. The bird beat the ground and lay on the peat with its wings spread wide. It was as if the earth had lifted itself up and headed for the heavens. I ran to finish the bird off. The shot had gone through the middle of its belly as it had raised itself to fly, and the job was quickly done. Guðmundur had hit three with his Belgian muck spreader.

The horse trembled, alarmed by the reports. We put the fleece on its back, carrying the birds and the guns as we led it through the marsh. It was still skittish after the blasts as we came up to the bank. I could feel that my feet had sunk into the bog. We were both muddy and Guðmundur was also wet. Sigurður took the horse and we walked back to the farmhouse where we hung the birds high on the barn wall so the dogs wouldn't sniff around them.

Sigurður invited us in and I dug through my bag for the cognac to give him. We drank coffee in the kitchen, bringing with us mud from the marsh onto the farmer's wife's white-scrubbed floor. It was warm inside after the spring wind and the housewife had a drink with us. They had two boys who ran outside to see the birds. We chatted about weather and crops. Later we went out again to see if there were more birds to be had.

6

The birds were with the guns in the back and there was quiet in the car apart from the rumble of the road beneath our wheels. By now it was late and we had made several visits to the shooting grounds. There were no more geese on the marsh and we watched them pass over, waiting for them as evening drew on, but they didn't settle.

We drove out of Hvalfjörður, over the Laxá River, into the Kjós district and from the high ground we could see the city lights merge into one in the dusk, like a white blanket laid over the point.

She came to me with the lights, and there was a powerful, warm sense of her that came suddenly. I could feel her heartbeat, her skin and her face through the city lights, knowing that she would be somewhere among them.

'It's quite a sight,' Guðmundur said.

'Yes,' I said.

'Have you been up here in the rain?'

'No, never when it's raining,' I said.

'The lights look different through the rain.'

'They're a fine sight for a traveller.'

'Like now,' he said.

'Yes. Just like now,' I said.

'Because the woman's there?'

'Among other things.'

'And now you'll be going to meet her.'

'Well…' I said.

'You take care.'

'I'll do my best.'

'So it doesn't turn out like it did with Kristín and Björg and…'

'That'll do,' I said.

'Sorry,' he said.

'Some of us know right from the start that these things come to an end.'

'That's a very sad thought,' he said.

'And wait for it to be over,' I said.

'You think it'll go that way?' he said.

'Perhaps there's never any other way,' I said.

The landscape was flat and in shadow out here, with no lights at any of the farms. As there were more dwellings along the road, there were more lights and before long we were in the outskirts and then driving along Suðurlandsbraut in the traffic and the blaring of horns. We drove around the square and across the street into the car park. Guðmundur waited in the car while I went into the office. There were a few people in the waiting room and the occasional call through the loudspeaker. Eiríkur came and asked where I had been, and when I told him he didn't believe me, and had to go out into the car park to find out if I was telling the truth. The others went to find out if I was telling lies, and I went to the phone box to call her. I flipped through the phone book to find Ólafur Faxen and dialled the number. I looked at the scribbles on the call box walls, listening to the phone ring, and it was so hot waiting there that my palms began to sweat. It rang for a long time before she answered.

I asked how she was and she replied that she felt fine, and I told her I had been up in Borgarfjörður hunting geese. I stretched the truth and said I had shot two and asked if she'd like one of them. She asked if I was serious and I told her, sure. She said that was sweet of me, and would I bring them now? I said I would. We said good-bye, and the receiver was wet in my hand, it was so hot in the phone box. I went to the bathroom to wash my hands. Through the porthole window I could see Hæi and Eiríkur admiring the geese. Guðmundur was there with them, giving them an impression of me with the fleece over my shoulders, which made them laugh. He could just wait until I came out and showed them how he had crept across the marsh with the horse. I went out into the car park where they all were.

'Isn't that sad,' Eiríkur said.

'What is?' Hæi said

'Killing birds,' Eiríkur said. He had one in his hands and stroked its neck and down to the broad white breast.

'Is that giving you a thrill?' I said.

'Killing them shouldn't be allowed,' Hæi said.

'You can be a disgrace, and you should be ashamed of yourself,' Eiríkur said.

'You ought to go square up,' Hæi said.

'That's taking things too far,' Guðmundur said.

'He's a bird-fancier.'

'What's that?'

'He wants to do it with the bird.'

'I thought it was some kind of hunting technique,' Hæi said.

'Hæi can be damnably stupid,' Eiríkur said.

'You didn't know what it meant either,' Hæi said.

Guðmundur sat in the car and Eiríkur placed the bird on the floor in the back.

'You should have seen him with the horse,' I said, imitating Guðmundur hiding behind the animal.

'I can well believe that you two must have been a sight worth seeing,' Eiríkur said.

I went round to the other side and sat in the front, and the others made their way out of the parking lot and back into the office.

'Bye, boys,' Eiríkur said.

We drove off and Guðmundur asked if I was going home. I told him that I needed to stop off on the way. He asked where and I told him it was the Faxen building. He gave me a sharp look, but I couldn't see his eyes in the shadows in the car, and neither could I see his face clearly. I could feel his gaze on me, which was both uncomfortable and overwhelming. He went back to watching the road and we drove on in silence.

'It's Guðríður Faxen?' he said.

'She lives there.'

'And that's who you're going to see?' he said, his voice deep, concerned and pained.

'You know Guðríður Faxen?' I said.

'No.'

'Then what?'

'Nothing.'

We drove past the harbour and saw that the wind was picking up, with spray carried across the road.

'Are you going to her?' he said.

'Yes.'

'You went inside to call her?'

'I told her I'd shot two birds.'

'And you want to give her two?'

'I'd like to. If that's all right with you.'

'Take them all.'

'No.'

'They'll spoil otherwise.'

'Fair enough. I'll give them to her with Guðmundur's respects.'

'No.'

'Why not?'

'You can do your own flirting with that upper-class whore of yours.'

'Why do you say that?'

'They're all like that.'

'You don't know the woman.'

'Fair enough.'

'Or maybe you do know her?'

'No.'

'I reckon it's taking things too damned far to call her a whore.'

'I didn't really mean it.'

The car pulled up outside the shop where I took the birds and thanked him for them. I told him I'd walk home, and he gave me a thin smile. I could see he regretted what he had said. His black car rolled away down the street and I knew he would be watching me in the mirror. A couple were walking in the other direction and by the time I went inside, they had already passed by. The lights were bright in the stairwell and up to the landing, where she had heard me coming and had opened the door, waiting for me. It was heart-warming to see her standing there in the door. She was going to take the birds, but I said I'd carry them for her and we went down to the basement where we put them on an empty biscuit box. They lay on their backs, necks hanging over the edge of the box. Their wings lay folded close to their breasts and the congealed blood was dark red against the white plumage.

'They're like fine gentlemen dressed in their best,' she said.

'Except for the blood.'

'The two go together, death and blood.'

'Especially with birds that have been shot.'

'I imagine the same would apply to fine gentlemen.'

'No.'

'All the same, they can bleed.'

'Not really.'

'Yes, but them bleeding wouldn't be a pretty sight.'

'Is anything bleeding pretty?'

'Your birds.'

'They're your birds now.'

'Our birds.'

We went back up the stairs and into the kitchen. She asked if I was hungry and I said I'd like a glass of milk. There was mud on my trousers and I could see my clothes were filthy after all that stalking. She stood by the bench by the sink and I told her about the hunt. I put the glass aside.

'Do you often shoot birds?' she asked

'Sometimes.'

'Does your friend enjoy it?' she said.

'He's a keen hunter.'

'But you aren't?'

'No.'

'I have a feeling that you are.'

'I'm sure I'm not.'

She was very close to me now. I could see her cheeks, the eyes with the flecks of gold around the pupils and her blue earrings.

'I think you are,' she said.

I saw her white teeth, and suddenly I couldn't focus on her face, just her lips moving as if she were about to say something, maybe once more that she was sure I was a great hunter. And then she was in my arms, pressed tight against me. The tap dripped, and I could hear the drops, until they stopped and the only thing was her, with her hands at my neck and running through my hair.

'It's so good that you came back,' she said.

'A man tries to be proud, but can't always be.'

'I wish I had your pride.'

'And a man doesn't want to steal another man's things, tries not to hurt anyone along the way or cause any pain, but can't always manage that.'

'That's true,' she said.

'And now I should be going.'

'No. Don't go.'

'At any rate, this has to stop.'

'Don't talk of stopping anything.'

'Talking about it maybe doesn't make any difference.'

'And don't think about it.'

'That can't be helped.'

'We'll be together for the time being, and if it ends, then it's no longer now.'

'That makes it harder to part.'

'No.'

'Let's be sensible,' I said.

'Yes, because life's so short.'

'I meant a different kind of sensible.'

'In that case, we shouldn't be. Let's be stupid and foolish, but not lonely.'

'It's wonderful to have found you.'

'And I'm so happy that you're back,' she said.

We were leaning against the bench, and I didn't feel comfortable making love in the kitchen. I asked if I could take a bath as I was muddy from the marshes. She ran a bath and gave me a dressing gown of her husband's, and some of his pyjamas to wear. Apart from the awkwardness of wearing her husband's night clothes and robe, it was as good as being married. There was a coolness to lying on the bed after the heat of the bathtub and there was a scent of her perfume to the duvet and the pillows. She emptied the bath and I heard her pottering in the kitchen. Then the phone in the hallway rang and I heard her answer it, saying that something wasn't possible, and repeating that no, it wasn't possible, and once more that it couldn't be done. I heard her put the receiver down in irritation. Then she came in, put out the light and undressed in the gloom. It wasn't all that dark, and she asked me to turn away. Maybe she was shy now there was no whisky. As I lay there with my back turned, she came to me under the bedclothes and the quiet of the night time was all around us.

7

As the days became warmer it was always a long time to wait for night to fall. It felt like going to church, going up those stairs, ringing the bell and seeing her standing there, the door opening and the red curtains behind her, and then the night.

Then there was the brightness in her bedroom, and her next to me with her dark hair loose, sleeping with her mouth open, which she said had been a habit that went back to childhood; falling asleep by her side, waking up with her and hearing the cathedral bells tolling in the town and the street bright and silent outside. We were engrossed in each other, sometimes going to the kitchen for a drink of milk or juice, but never whisky, that was something we never needed to stoke our passion between the sheets. We never spoke of bringing things between us to an end, and neither did we mention that her husband's operation was due to take place in July. Only her mother reminded us of that. She stayed with Gógó at weekends, which is why we never spent Saturdays and Sundays together, just Monday and the other weekdays and nights.

She said that she went with her mother to visit acquaintances, sitting and chatting, often well into the night which she found a burden. So by Monday she would be tired and sleepy, and not much in the mood for love. I developed a dislike for her mother, that she should tire her out so completely, and that she was the one who reminded me that Gógó had a husband who could yet make an appearance and end everything between us.

I used to walk to her place, so the car wouldn't be seen outside to give the neighbours something to be suspicious about. I used to leave the car in a parking lot, except for a week when it was in the garage and as far as the boys were concerned, I spent my nights at home.

By June Guðmundur was spending a lot of time out of town, so we met rarely and now that it was summer we no longer played chess. It was a bleak outlook for us city drivers who were either shut inside our cars or else waiting on the rank to hurry back behind the wheel to the smell of petrol, exhaust fumes and the endless din, far from the peace of cool shadows with white sunshine outside and the longed-for cold green pine freshness. Every fibre in us was telling us to get away, as others were becoming brown in the sun, breathing in the smell of a sea of blossom and warm blue skies, and the warmth of the land in shades of earth-brown, sparkling green and pale white.

Guðmundur's car was a newer one, which allowed him to get away, telling us of trips to the east and the west, and in between he was working like the others who had better cars. From around the end of May onwards the rest of us began to see the difference a new car made for those who were able to get away from the rat race. By June it was obvious and rankled constantly. We tried to forget all this with the occasional dram, but it only made our ramshackle old cars even harder to work with as they continued to rattle when it was hot out, when everything was merciless and bare, and the atmosphere of the city was like a long-drawn out scream.

In June there were a good few fares down south to the military base and although there was good money in it, we didn't see much of a summer; and nothing would replace it for us, and certainly not the girls hardly more than teenagers, who felt they were living the life by travelling with some soldiers along the dusty Keflavík road. It was like the occupation years during the war, except that there were more roads that had come to an end with tearful partings by a dock; no different to the pain of trying to forget.

If it wasn't Keflavík by night and morning all through that month of June's weekends, it was fares around the town's cinemas and dance halls. My thoughts often went to them, out there on the highway, while I was waiting for Cab 79 to be called up, or seventy-nine whatever.

It was always good to see Guðmundur when he was between fares, and if we didn't talk about cars then we'd discuss politics but he never mentioned Gógó, just as if she had never been the cause any bitterness between us. He was deeply opposed to the military presence, and we didn't always agree on that.

I told him a few of the things I had been seen back then, and some of it wasn't good, not comfortable things to be hearing, and the others who weren't out of town saw the same stuff. If this was anything to go by, then we could as well give up on being an independent people, and I feel that he understood that things weren't as black as they were in our eyes.

So the days passed without much by the way of excitement, except that six men were arrested for moonshining at the end of the month. These were measures being taken because of the National Day, because they thought we had been responsible for public drunkenness on the seventeenth of June. I was one of the six and this was the first time I had been in any trouble. Moonshining wasn't anything to make a fuss over, although the papers did. When I told Gógó I had been arrested she thought I had been upset and wanted us to leave town for a few days. Because my car was in the garage at the end of the month there was nothing to stop me taking time off, so we drove out to Thingvellir in her Buick and stayed there for a night. The next day we took a boat out onto the lake and I taught her to row. Out there at Thingvellir wasn't a comfortable place for us to be, except out on the lake and upstairs in the hotel room where we could be at ease. And on the way back in the Buick that evening we decided that we wouldn't again try and go anywhere to be like other people.

8

It was late at night when I rolled into town and went straight to bed. It had been a long and tiring trip out past the mountains to the east with a pair of drunks who had spent the day searching for people they thought were their friends, but who weren't any such thing, and were pushy about imposing themselves wherever they went. They were painfully polite and unctuous, drinking the whole time, talking petulantly about their ancestry, and how people who hadn't given them a chance had stolen their ideas to become big wheels at their expense. It was the middle of the week and things had been quiet, and although the pair hadn't been the most pleasant passengers, they paid their fare and it was a healthy amount.

The sun had stopped shining into my room when my landlady came and woke me up. I had slept through the morning and past midday. She had a letter for me from home and said she reckoned I ought to be on my feet.

When I got to the rank I read the letter once I'd hung my number on the board. It was from the old lady, and as always, I was her darling boy. She asked what I was doing, as if she didn't know that I was driving this bitch of a car. I could feel her sneer as I read the letter. Although it was written in a tone that told me just how much I had let her down by leaving home, it was still good to hear from her. She included all the details of what was going on at home, how the cows were milking and what colour the calves were. She told me about the horses, knowing I had a liking for them. But she had less to say about the horses than the cattle. She was more fond of them. Sometimes she'd give me a lecture about corruption and loose morals, even though the only experience she had of either was through the pages of the Old Testament, and pulp literature like *the Secrets of Paris*. In every letter she repeated her desire that I'd get myself married.

There was nobody in the waiting room except Eiríkur and he had nothing to say about me reading a letter. He didn't ask if it was from a married woman or if someone up north reckoned I'd fathered a child there. It was unusual that he didn't make his presence felt, maybe because the others weren't there.

Eiríkur came to sit next to me and I stuffed the letter into my pocket.

'Number three hundred and four,' the girl said through the loudspeaker.

We sat on the leather seats of the bench that was up against the wall. He gave me a smoke and was very quiet. It occurred to me to ask if there was something troubling him. Eiríkur lay down on the bench with his feet trailing on the floor, so I decided against asking anything and read the newspaper instead.

There was plenty of news in the papers. I read that it had been hot in Europe, but not the same as here. Now the weather was close and the first five days of July had been cool. According to the local news there had been two burglaries and one fatal accident, and little herring to be found off the north coast. Haymaking had begun in most districts and the trawlers weren't doing badly. Politics seemed to be doing pretty well. I read everything there was about the fatal accident.

'Do you know whose registration number that is, Eiríkur?' I said.

'What?'

I repeated the number.

'That's my car's number,' he said and stared at the wall. I wished I hadn't asked him and knew that it would be unbearable for him in the silence. He could be cocky, but he was a decent fellow. Now I understood that this was what troubled him and he would break down if I were to try to lighten his misery with something trivial.

'It was me who did it,' he said, eyes fixed on the wall.

'A hundred and fourteen,' the girl announced.

'You're being called, Eiríkur,' one of the other drivers said.

He didn't reply, staying where he was, lying on the bench and staring at the wall.

She called the number three times and then two hundred and eighty-eight. Her voice was thin and sharp, with a catch to it that was as irritating as the muttering among the drivers. I could feel the overbearing noise of both, while he was next to me and was the worse off of us for being Eiríkur.

'Take it easy,' I said.

'He was only seven,' he said, hiding his face in the corner where the bench met the wall. The girl called another number over the loudspeaker. The room was brown up to the middle of the wall, light yellow from there up and the ceiling was the same colour.

'Try not to think about it. I know it must be painful, but don't think about it,' I said.

'He was only seven.'

'It could happen to anyone,' I said, knowing it was no comfort to him. Nothing but time would be any help to him, or if he were that way inclined, there was always God.

The girl's voice came over the loudspeaker and this time it was my number. I stood up and left the waiting room. When I was back from my fare to the airport, Eiríkur was gone and they said he had hung his number on the board and was out.

Guðmundur came in. He had been out of town for the last two days. Then Hæi came in a little later. We talked about the accident and they said that the boy had run in front of the car. It was awkward when

Eiríkur came back, and he sensed that we had been discussing the accident as everyone fell suddenly silent and there was nothing else to talk about for the moment. After that we made an effort to be cheerful and upbeat but that didn't go well, so we tried a few dirty jokes, but nobody was in the mood to do it properly. Some of us read the papers to make it look as if we weren't thinking about the accident.

I had a couple of fares and had a meal at the canteen around seven. The waitress confided in me that she would be leaving soon and was going to be married, but Guðmundur, Róbert and I were the ones she would miss. She wasn't worried about any of the others. I told her what had happened to Eiríkur and she replied that he was a decent guy in spite of everything, and maybe it would be Guðmundur, me, Róbert and Eiríkur she would miss. There had been a phone call while I had been out for dinner. Then I didn't get another fare until almost eight and it was half-past when I was back, to find a note saying that I was to call Gógó.

I took the scrap of paper and put it in my pocket. Things were busy and I thought I'd call after nine when there would be a break and a chance to talk to her in peace and quiet. There were four ahead of me in the queue and one after another they were called out. Now there was only one left besides me in the waiting room and both numbers were on the rack at reception.

'Seventy-nine, would you please come to the phone,' the loudspeaker announced.

The girl had a habit of saying 'would you please come to the phone' and 'would you please take a message' and 'would you please' do this or that. I wondered if she invited her boyfriends to 'would you please…' and a few other ugly thoughts about her because now I'd lose my place in the queue.

Gógó was on the line and her voice was strange. Maybe she had been drinking some of that bourgeois whisky of hers. She sounded a little irritable.

'You're not an easy man to get hold of,' she said.

'I was at work.'

'Didn't you get my message asking you to call?' she asked.

'Sure. But it's been busy and I was going to call you after nine.'

'So you can't call when I ask you to?' she said.

I didn't feel like arguing with her over the phone. Then the girl called up my number, as if she didn't know I was on the phone as she had only just told me to take a call.

'Is there something wrong?' I asked.

She didn't answer.

'Hello?' I said, to see if she was still there.

'Come to me,' she said and now there was no irritation in her voice, just sadness.

'What's the matter?' I asked.

'Come,' she said.

'Isn't it all right if I come after nine?' I said.

'Come now,' she said and there was the click of the receiver being dropped into its cradle.

I went out into the waiting room and meant to hang my number on the board. But why be so proud? In reality, all pride was such a small thing that had become ridiculous and impersonal since May and all the way until now in July. Pride was for those who could live on that alone.

There was someone who wanted to hang up his number ahead of me, and I let him.

To be a man, to experience both the good and the bad and survive both, you can't be proud, quick to be offended and reckless without seeing the amusing side of your fellow man. Someone else came long to hang his number on the rack.

'Aren't you putting your number up, Ragnar?' he said.

'Hell, no.'

'What? I was only asking.'

Maybe that's not the way it was, but rather how it was for the others who wanted you to be a decent fellow. It wasn't pleasant to be dropped into such a role, and uncomfortable afterwards to know that this was something that suited skirt-chasers, painted ladies and bazaar people. But Gógó was none of these. Something bad had certainly happened to her. I went out to the car. It was busy and before long they wouldn't be going into the waiting room, but simply driving up to the rank and being handed their next fare without even having to get out of the car.

I drove out of the lot, crossed over the street and down to the harbour. There wasn't a breath of wind, and there were a few ships there. The customs cutter was chugging past out by the lighthouse. I drove up to the house and pulled up sharply behind the Buick. I rang the bell and she came to the door right away, and I could see she had been crying.

'What's the matter?' I said and closed the door.

She said nothing, but turned away and went into the living room. I followed and she threw herself on the couch. She lay there curled up with only the back of her head, her shoulders and feet to be seen.

'He's dead,' she said.

Standing there I didn't know whether to be delighted or sorrowful. This was one more injury I'd caused this man, as I was clearly not saddened at his death. I felt that the colours in the living room had brightened and I wanted to laugh. I sat down and looked at Gógó.

'He was a good man,' she said from where she lay on the couch.

Seeing her and hearing her say this was painful, as if she had just realised that he was gone. I stood up and went into the other room. There was a picture of him there. He had a gentler look on his face than in the picture of him she had shown me that first night I spent with her. There was a dignity to him in this one

74

that had been lacking in the other picture. There was no missing his scar, deep enough for it to be a shadow in the photograph. I heard her behind me.

'That's right. Look at him,' she said in a voice that was so odd and overwrought that I hardly recognised it, as if instead of the person I knew, she had become a stranger. I said nothing and went to the window to look out over the garden. There were leaves on the tree, heavy with sap, that shivered in the breeze. That's the growth that's there in everything that's born and everything that dies. And did anything ever die other than to be reborn, so what reason is there for sorrow over what's inevitable? Do the leaves know that they turn blood red at the end of their lives, and they are never so beautiful as they are just then; that death and life come from the same beauty, that without life there would be no death, and that life would be a greater sorrow than itself; even though a person stands like a hundred metre sprinter at the starting line, ready with all his sentimental heart filled with sadness as death comes to finish things off.

'Do you have anything to drink?' she asked.

'I have some akvavit, but unfortunately there's no whisky, nor is there any champagne, even though you'd probably have chosen that over the other options,' I said.

I immediately regretted trying to hurt her. Maybe the picture had made me spiteful towards her because she was in pain. Maybe she was turning us each

75

against the other to be sure that she was mourning the death of this lost man, who had in fact left long ago and had not known that she was still in this world that he was leaving.

'You don't need to be bitter. He's never coming back,' she said.

I gazed out into the garden. It all felt deeply unreal. All the same, I had feared the day he might return. Now I understood fully that there was nothing to fear any longer; that I would no longer have to wake in the night as a guest in a strange house, waiting for a man in Denmark to regain his health.

'I'm not bitter. It's because you told me to look at him, as if I ought to be asking his forgiveness.'

'We should both be asking his forgiveness.'

'Why?' I said.

'Now that he's dead, I feel like a whore,' she said.

'Is that what we have together?' I said.

'No, but there's so much else that hasn't been that way.'

I said I'd go and fetch the akvavit. She was much calmer when I returned. I asked her to sit down and said I'd fetch glasses and water from the kitchen. I fussed for a while, letting the water run cold, getting glasses and opening the bottle. The water was cold by the time I mixed our drinks. I mixed them weak, and she asked me to make it stronger once she had taken a sip and I poured more akvavit into her glass. We sat for a while saying nothing, drinking akvavit and water.

'Did he die during the operation?' I asked.

'No. He wasn't due to have surgery until the fifteenth.'

'You heard about this today?'

'Yes. Just before I called you the first time.'

'And he died today?'

'He died at two o'clock.'

'Maybe it's for the best.'

'What do you mean?'

'The surgery might have gone badly.'

'You can't tell.'

'Can't we talk about this sensibly?'

'You can't. I think you're pleased.'

'More akvavit,' I said.

She wanted another glass.

'I'm truly sorry,' I said.

'You don't care.'

'How do you want me to be so you can be satisfied?'

'I don't know.'

She went into the bedroom and I heard her throw herself onto the bed, and heard as well that she was crying. I poured myself more akvavit and and waited for her to be calm. It was a good while before I could no longer hear her crying. I went in to her, sat on the bed and placed a hand on her shoulder.

'Don't touch me,' she said.

I withdrew my hand, sat on the bed and looked out past the drawn curtains to the living room beyond.

'Don't blame yourself. It won't make any difference or save his life. And if you've done anything you think you need to atone for because of him, then it's too late. It's an honourable thing to mourn him, just as it's pointless for you to be playing a role in his death.'

She sat up quickly and slapped my face hard. My nose hurt and I put a hand over it. She stared at me with her eyes wide.

'Do you feel better now?' I said.

She lay back on the bed.

'Get me some akvavit,' she said.

I went into the living room to fetch a glass and handed it to her. She drank some of it and passed it back to me.

'I'm a scoundrel,' she said.

'Don't go blaming yourself.'

'It's true. I'm a scoundrel,' she said with determination. 'I married him for his money. I didn't love him and I was relieved when he went mad and I didn't have to sleep with him any longer.'

'You're lovely,' I said and handed her the glass.

She got up off the bed and stood in front of me with the glass in her hand.

'Take me right here on the carpet that he gave me because he loved me. Take me because I'm a gold digger and because I'm a bitch and a scoundrel.'

The carpet was red and thick, patterned in yellow. I looked up from it at her.

'You're being very dramatic,' I said.

Her hand moved in an arc, and it was cold and my eyes stung as the drink in her glass was thrown in my face. I heard her stride out of the room while I wiped my face. I followed behind her and sat next to her on the couch. My face was still wet from being splashed.

'You shouldn't waste akvavit,' I said.

She turned to me and it was as if her face suddenly thawed out. She moved close and asked me to put my arms around her. I did so and she sobbed into my chest. There was a warm, familiar smell to her hair. Once her sobs had faded away I handed her a handkerchief to blow her nose.

'Do you love me?' she asked, her voice nasal and heavy after her tears.

'Very much,' I said.

'My love. Say it. My love.'

'My love,' I said.

'I wish I could be as calm as you are.'

'You're lovely and I'm certainly not calm.'

'Yes, my darling. You're calm and you have good shoulders for crying on.'

'They're there for when you're sad.'

'Always, my love. Say that it will be always.'

The phone rang out in the passage and she went to answer it. I poured myself more akvavit while she was talking on the phone and I kicked off my shoes to make myself comfortable.

9

The rain on the car's windscreen fell in torrents, splashed aside by the rapid sweep of the wiper as the engine idled. I had been to the canteen and there was a new girl there. This one didn't have the farmer's wife look of her predecessor, the homely air she had about her or our shared love of food. It was strange to sit on one of the stools with this young woman on the other side. I waited for the place to empty out and for them all to drive over to the rank for their fares, which would be pretty much right now. Because it was raining it had been an unusually busy afternoon for a Saturday, and I had already taken two hundred krónur in fares. The rain continued to fall on the car and to beat a steady rhythm on the street by the parking lot. The falling drops painted the glittering asphalt an unbroken rainbow in the shape of the street, from the pavement on the other side to the entrance to the lot.

The regular loud pulsing of the wiper, the rain falling on the street and the drops hitting the car were enough to send a man to sleep.

I had not seen Gógó for two weeks. Then she had called today to say that now everything would be fine, that her mother would be leaving at the weekend.

Every now and then drivers would come running from the waiting room, coats held tight against them and got hurriedly into their cars before driving off fast out of the lot, shivering at the sight of all that water.

Ólafur Faxen's body had been brought home by ship and I had been down in Keflavík the day he was buried. He had been given a respectable funeral. I didn't call Gógó then, or while she had waited for his body to be returned. A car splashed along the street and stopped in front so I no longer saw the pooling water on the pavement, only the raindrops falling on the windscreen and the bonnet. If he was going to stop there, then I'd have to back up to get to the rank. While I sat there hoping he'd move along, I saw the driver wind down his window. He looked at me, glanced from side to side and then back to me. His hair was wet with rain and he squinted against the downpour. He drove for another firm and I didn't know what he was up to, and hoped he'd be on his way. The wiper on his side of the windscreen swept the water away faster than the one on my side, and at intervals they'd be in time with each other. The man ran from his car, over to me and pulled open the passenger door. Rain fell on the seat while he was getting in and finally pulled the door shut behind him. I could see a film of water on his face and drops had collected on the collar of his jacket.

'I'm after some whisky,' he said.

'On your own?'

'Yes,' he said.

'Anything in particular?'

82

'Scotch,' he said.

'Posh people?'

'Hell, no,' he said.

'They want whisky?'

'Nothing else. I have gin and cognac. It's a proper nuisance.'

All the cars had left the parking lot and the rain pattered onto the bare paving, cracked and sunken here and there, and the rain bucketed onto the dark, wet north wall of the rank, windowless apart from the porthole in the toilet.

'Who's so fussy?' I said.

'Bill.'

'Bill what?'

'He's an American.'

'You know him well?' I said.

'He's all right.'

'And the people with him?'

'That's his girlfriend.'

'She's all right?'

'I'll vouch for them both, if you have a bottle.'

'How about on your rank?'

'Nobody there has any whisky.'

'I'll have to go home to fetch it.'

'Please do. You'll get me out of a fix.'

'Who's his squeeze?'

'She's a widow, or divorced, or something.'

'That's cosy.'

'He spends Saturdays and Sundays with her.'

'I see you're keeping tabs.'

'Don't you do any Yank business?'

'Not a lot.'

'You ought to get into it.'

'You sell them quite a bit?'

'Sometimes, but then they bring their own as well,' he said.

'It's cheaper for them that way.'

'It's a big difference,' he said.

'Where do I take the bottle?'

'To the Faxen House. Stop outside and sound your horn.'

'The Faxen House, you said?'

'You know, where the shop is,' he said and was smiling as he opened the door. The rain swept in and a draught blew through the car. He got out and turned around, holding the door open. I watched him lift the collar of his jacket.

'You'll sort it out?' he said.

'I'll sort it out.'

He slammed the door and I saw him walk away from the car and run across the rainswept parking lot, splashing through the puddles and his clothes darkening with damp on the side that faced the weather. I sat numb, my thoughts frozen as he ran across to his own car and drove off. After that there was nothing but the street and the cars driving along it, spraying water from under their wheels through the pools down by the rank. I started the engine, and drove out of the lot into the traffic trying to not think about what I had heard. All the same, I could feel it at the back of my mind, dark, bitter and oppressive, and there was a lump in my throat. It was there as well in the rhythm of the wipers and the rain pattering on the road and the growl of the engine. My mind went around in circles, and I kept coming back to the same conclusion as I drove home, the circles tightening and closer and in between them were the Faxen House and Gógó and all the weekends when she had said it was her mother there. Then there was the emptiness that was where she had been. Then no more of her, and none of all this, but around in a circle arriving at the same emptiness, until the emptiness and the thought was exhausted and there was no pain left in it.

The rain was thinning, and the water was flowing off the tarmac and into the gutters by the pavements. I slowed the wipers and there was a restfulness to their steady beat.

I couldn't leave the car on the same side of the road as the house, so I crossed the street with the chill rain on my hair, opened the heavy door and took the stairs at a run. There were three children on the bottom landing who called out to me. They were the children of the couple on the first floor, and I sometimes gave them some chocolate. I tried to say something pleasant, and carried on up. It was cold in my room, filled with a grey light. The bedclothes lay

85

on the sofa bed where I had left them, and the chair's brown upholstery was the colour of earth in the light that the green curtains failed to add any warmth to. I went to the wardrobe for whisky. It was a bottle of Vat 69 and I wrapped paper around the cold glass and carried the package down the stairs, past the children and over to the car. I could hear the calls of the children out on the street. By now the rain had practically stopped. I turned the key and put my foot on the starter. It turned over sluggishly, so I lifted my foot, and tried again. The engine could be heard turning over, but wouldn't fire. I put my foot down hard on the starter, but the engine was dead.

I could feel my bitterness flooding through the emptiness, and recalled every detail, the arrogance, the smugness, strutting of those I had ferried as they tried to be something higher and better educated, part of the upper class, even when they needed to piss and spew; that my year in this city had been nothing but this old car, booze and fleeting flings with women who had glossy pictures of Tyrone Power, Robert Taylor and Farley Granger by the headboard. I gave the starter a rest, and switched the key a few times to make sure there was a connection. It hurt to feel that things were coming to a climax, the failure inside and the regret at not having tried to escape the endless and doomed passing of years in the city, to be a person and not just a machine steering this old car; to have grass under my feet instead of tarmac, and animals and their pride and majesty instead of the engine and cold iron. I stepped on the starter and it spun fast, becoming a howl of cogs as the cylinders started to fire, until the engine was running and the spring spat the cogs off. I put the car into gear. The bottle in its paper wrapping lay on the seat beside me. I turned out of the street, a hand on the bottle so it wouldn't roll off, and drove down the main street behind the other cars and waited at a red light until it turned green. Then it was along the main street and past two sets of lights. The Buick was parked by the door and it occurred to me that this was the third time I had parked behind it. I put my right thumb on the horn ring and pressed three times. There was a sharp tone from the horn. While I waited I read the Buick's number again and again to settle myself. A man came out of the house, and hesitated in the doorway. He wasn't in uniform, but in a gabardine outfit that suited him, blue and he seemed nothing out of the ordinary, maybe because I had expected him to be in uniform. He wore a grey shirt and his hair was cut very short. I couldn't see his shoes and he slowly approached my side of the car. I wound down the window. He looked and me and was very awkward. His eyes were grey and I saw that he had pitted cheeks. He wasn't drunk and it was obvious he didn't know what to say because I wasn't the other driver.

'I brought your bottle.'

He smiled amiably and sat in the back.

'Where's Bjössi?' he said.

'Bjössi didn't have any whisky, so he asked me to let you have this,' I said and passed the bottle in its paper wrapping over the back of the front seat. He took the package, holding it by the neck of the bottle.

'What sort of whisky is it?' he said.

'Vat 69,' I said.

'That's fine. Very, very good whisky,' he said.

'The best,' I said.

'How much?' he said.

'A hundred and eighty-five,' I said. He took out his wallet. There were pictures in it in plastic sleeves. He handed me a hundred and ninety.

'Make it a hundred and ninety-five,' I said.

'Why?'

'Delivery,' I said.

'You said a hundred and eighty-five and that's what I'll pay.'

'Give me the bottle.'

'Take it easy, old man.'

'I'm no old man, and you give me that bottle back.'

'You're sure?'

'All right. Get out.'

'Sure, old man,' he said and held the bottle close. I opened the door for him. As I reached back for the door handle, he raised the hand that wasn't holding the bottle and clenched his fist. Then he saw I was opening the door and he quickly opened his hand,

88

extending it as if to be shaken. I shook my head and he shrugged his shoulders as he got out. The gears rattled as I put the car into gear. He slammed the door and I drove away quickly, leaving him standing on the pavement. They would drink the whisky, and after that they would… Just imagine you've never seen the woman. If you can't do that, imagine her as nothing, think of her as an old woman or picture her as fat. Tell yourself that a few times, and that she looks down on you, that there was nothing special about being in bed with her, that she had asthma, or some such crap. For Christ's sake, stand up straight, be a man. Oh, shut your mouth. You know it's all a lie, that you'll never get her out of your blood or forget those nights.

There wasn't much traffic, as it had stopped raining and now there were a good few cars in the lot. I went into the waiting room. Four of them were there playing blackjack at the long table. I hung my number up. They were making plenty of noise.

'The usual,' the players bantered.

'Play a card, you pillock.'

'Drop the bastard.'

'Here's Culbertson.'

'Right you are.'

'Queen o' clubs.'

'One o' diamonds.'

'Keep it coming.'

'And another one.'

'I thought as much.'

'And the king of hearts.'

I watched them engrossed in the cards. There were two calls over the loudspeaker; a man's voice this time. The girl was on holiday. His voice was gloomy and I could hear the man's heavy breathing. He said fifty-four off the rank, huffing before and after as he was too close to the microphone.

'Seventy-nine, you're wanted on the phone,' he said, and there was no huffing now, and there was no 'if you please' like the girl always said.

I went around and was told the call had been put through to the call box. I knew it was her the moment I put the receiver to my ear.

'Ragnar,' she said and there was a clarity to her voice, as there is among those who have watched an accident and aren't ready to accept it was as they saw it happen.

'Yes,' I said.

'Ragnar, I saw the car.'

'What car?'

'Your car. Just now. Outside here.'

'That must have been some other car,' I said, reading the graffiti scrawled on the wall. There was filth and people's names. I'd usually have found the filth revolting, but now it was as welcome as the gospel and there was a solace in reading it.

'No, Ragnar. It was you.'

'Not at all. I've only just got back to town and went straight to the rank,' I said.

'I was sure it was your car,' she said.

'I couldn't have been,' I said.

'But I thought it was.'

'Believe me.'

'Ragnar.'

'Yes?'

'You're a good man.'

Silence.

'And I'm a bad woman.'

Silence.

'And you have to remember that I never said I was a good woman.'

Silence.

'Ragnar.'

'Yes?'

'Soon... Soon we'll be together.'

'Yes.'

'And never part.'

'No.'

'Are you certain, Ragnar, that it wasn't you?'

'Absolutely.'

We said goodbye and I read no more of the filth on the wall. I went out to the toilet and threw up. Then I went back to the waiting room and went back to watching them play cards. Their hands fluttered over the table and faces grinned and grimaced, and their lips moved. I heard her voice, just as it had been over the phone, and her voice during the nights together and her laughter, and remembered how her breasts rose and fell when she laughed.

'I never get the right cards,' someone said over the card table.

'You get the jacks.'

And the night at Thingvellir, watching her resplendent beneath the window as we took in the landscape and its beauty, and saw the waves in the night breeze on the lake; gazing at the mountains in shadow and the moss-covered lava and being silent together, because that was everything. And being completely and beautifully content in bed, because the night and the mountains and the lake were there with us. Don't think of him there with her, and don't think that you've lost anything. All men die alone, even when only a part of them dies, and they have to accept it just as you're accepting this and that you keep living to be cut to pieces until it's all over.

Guðmundur wasn't there in the waiting room. It wasn't pleasant being there alone and I hoped he'd show up. I went out and to the back of the line of cars in the lot to my car and sat in it. It was cold in there so I started the engine and revved it so it would warm up faster. I turned up the heater. There could yet be a long wait for Guðmundur and I groped under the front seat for a bottle. I had no joy from drinking. The heater wasn't whining quite as loudly by the time I had taken a couple of swigs from the bottle and the rain started to fall again. The drops streamed down onto the bonnet and the windscreen. I didn't see Guðmundur drive into the parking lot. He had parked on my offside and as he walked past, he saw I was in the car and came over to me.

'Feel like a drink?' I said.

'What's up?'

'Nothing. Just asking if you want a drink.'

'Anything happened?'

'Hell, no. Why should it have?'

'Usually…'

'Forget that. My treat.'

'That's brennivín.'

'Isn't it good enough?'

'I thought you only drank whisky these days,' he said and it was cold, and it was good that he could make a joke.

I handed him the bottle.

10

The road streamed away behind the car, its speed twisting lengthways all of the road's lines. Even the shadows were skewed as they vanished under the pugnacious snout and the chrome ram on the bonnet cut through the night from where it was poised to leap from its place at the front of the panel that divided the two sides of the bonnet. My lips were swollen and sore. I had a pain deep in my belly from where he had beaten me, but it was less now than when I had lain in the parking lot between the cars, knees drawn up to my chin to lessen the pain. It had been a foul fight, and a meaningless one. It was like hitting myself each time I landed a blow on him, and it was as well that he fought back properly, with adroitness and immediate results, until the others came to pull us apart. They took him to one side, holding him and standing with him as I lay there curled in a ball.

He told them there was no need to hold him back, and I saw him walk away from them and over to the car, where he leaned against it with his head in the crook of his elbow, hammering the car with his fists and rolling his head as if he could find no respite. I saw him stumble from the car and across the lot over to his own, and he drove away as they stood over me and talked about calling a doctor. After that I got to my feet and went to the toilets.

He had said something about Gógó and I had punched him hard in the face. He had stared at me with his placid brown eyes as blood seeped from the corner of his mouth. I hit him a second time because it hurt so much to see him looking back like that.

I drove along the broad grey gravel road and into Kollafjörður, up the slope the other side, on past the bay further on and past the farms. There was no light out on the point and the city was still, cold and gloomy under a sky grey and heavy with rain.

An autumn day seven years before and the mountainsides had been sprinkled with snow during the night, when I drove into the taxi rank's parking lot. It had been early in the morning, with cold sunshine and few cars about, my first day at the rank and I had been a bag of nerves. Guðmundur had driven into the lot as I was fussing over the car and we walked together over to the waiting room. He told me to get a map of the city to drive by for the first few days. It had been quiet that morning and we finished a game of chess before lunch. He continued to keep an eye out for me, gave me advice and helped me over difficulties, even problems with other drivers.

The city away to my side had vanished from view. The road through the Kjós district was dry and hard, and after a while I was crossing the Laxá bridge. I took a slug from the bottle once I was on the far side.

He had lent me money when I couldn't meet the payments on the car, and he talked through things it was as well for me to know. Occasionally we'd drink together and did much else together.

It was getting on for one o'clock when I reached the bottom of Hvalfjörður and was past the bend on the outward stretch. There was plenty of gear shifting up and down the slopes and I took another swig from the bottle now and again. My lips had stopped swelling. I could feel that they were going to be sore next to my teeth, as could feel the sting every time I took a drink. There were two cars parked outside Ferstikla and it was good to be leaving Hvalfjörður behind. I went through the Leirár parish, took the road beneath the mountain of Hafnarfjall and saw that the clouds were hanging low over Borgarfjörður. The wind blew hard in the shadow of Hafnarfjall and needed a firm hand on the wheel in the storm-force gusts. As darkness fell the lights of Borgarnes could be made out on the other side of the water.

That hadn't always been an easy journey, especially that time with a passenger who hadn't been all that drunk, on his way one Easter Saturday to the old folks who lived some way outside the town. I hadn't known until afterwards that he had been after money from the old man. I found them in the cowshed, where the man was on top of the old boy in one of the stalls with a knife in his hand, threatening to kill the old man if he didn't get the money. There was dust in the old man's hair and he was turning his head back and forth. I stood there in the cowshed, listening to the man swearing and the old boy's groans, and I took the cowshed shovel and let the fellow have it on the head. Once I had dragged the guy out to the car I helped the old man out of the cowshed and into the farmhouse as he said again and again that he had no money.

I was past the Hvítá bridge by now, swung past the gravel hills, over the bridges crossing the streams and onward over the heights and down into the bay between the outcrops, all the way to where the road takes a sharp bend to the north. As I took the turn, I read the numbers on the road sign. There was a stretch from there where the road was soft, so the car didn't rattle as much but didn't keep the same speed as before. I drove down the slope and on through the marshlands, and then past Svígnaskarð. Then the road was harder once I was into lava territory where the moss and the lichens and the scorched black rocks took on brilliant colours in the night. My lips weren't so painful now, as long as I didn't move them. I could feel the stiffness in them, and it made it sore to drink from the bottle, and also because of the sting.

From the lava fields I emerged into farmlands. There were horses below the road and the Norðurá river was away to the right. It had been at my side all the way from the bend at Hólmavað. Sometimes it was a little distance away so that it was out of my sight, but it was good to know it was there travelling through the night on its way to the estuary. I passed quickly over the flatlands around Dalsmynni and had the rocky outcrop of Hraunsnef on my left and Baula ahead. It was under the sky here that Guðmundur had been a youngster, where he had seen the mountains in the mornings, feeling the solidity and permanence of them, and their purity when the winter fell, colouring and covering the land in white. I carried on through pastures and the flats, and took the corner up onto the Sanddalsá bridge. The terrain started to rise, then I was at Sveinatunga and before long it was behind me as I took the road under the cliffs. I took the Norðurá bridge where this old lady of a river was blue between the broken water down in the gorge.

My mind was calmer now and I rolled down the window to get some air into the car. I drove fast past the hills by Hellistungur. There wasn't much left in the tank and I'd have to wake someone up at Fornihvammur for fuel. I crossed the Norðurá river again, followed the side road and up the track up to the house. I took the track in second and it was as good as a rest to roll into the yard. It was getting on for three. I leaned on the horn and sounded it a couple of times. There was a chance it wouldn't be easy to get someone out and was reluctant to sound the horn too much and wake the whole house. I got out of the car and was going to go up to the house, but my feet were numb and I dropped back into the seat. I left the car door open with my feet outside on the ground and my elbow on the horn to sound it again. It was a still night, with only a few rags of clouds above the heath. It rose high in gentle waves that billowed from the lowlands on this side of the river which was pasture. I knew that there was flat land behind the first of the slopes. The road followed it that way before the bridge and up towards the high ground.

I heard a door shut behind me. The chatter of the river was carried to me through the still air and I looked away from the heath and back along the car. A youngster came across the yard. He was fair-haired, with hair thin on his crown, and wearing a shirt without a jacket. He came up to my side of the car.

'It's fuel you're after?' he said.

'Fill her up for me,' I said. He went round the back and I heard him rattle the chain on the tank. I stretched across the seat and pushed open the door so I could watch him pump fuel.

'How far to Blönduós?' I said, just to have something to say to the boy. He changed one hand on the pump for the other.

'Two hours,' he said, sizing up my ugly lips and I'm sure he thought I'd stolen the car. I could see in the wing mirror on the hood that there was swelling around one ear and around both eyes, and my lips were puffed and cut. It was obvious he found it suspicious to see someone looking like this on the road by night and up-country.

'I'm on my way home,' I said by way of explanation.

'Sure,' he said, disbelieving.

'Are you from here?' I said.

'I'm from the west,' he said.

'You never want to go home?'

'I go back now and again,' he said, changing hands again. There was a good amount in the tank by now. He changed hands one more time and I said that it had to be enough once he had pumped fifty-five litres. He asked if I'd come inside to get my receipt.

'I don't need a receipt,' I said.

'I have to write one out anyway.'

'Here's the cash.'

'I'll go and get your change,' he said.

'Keep it.'

He was surprised. It wasn't usual to tip someone who pumped fuel.

'You get to keep the change because the car likes it that way,' I said. 'It's from the car to you. You get me?'

'I won't be a moment getting your change,' he said.

'We don't want change. And have a dram to help you sleep,' I said, leaning over the seat for the bottle.

'No, thanks.'

'Fair enough.'

'Have you come far?'

'From Reykjavík.'

'And you're going up north?'

'To Skagafjörður.'

'You can stay the night here.'

'Not a chance, my friend.'

'You're tired,' he said.

'A man on the road home is never tired.'

'You're in no state to drive.'

'I'm fine.'

'Up to you.'

'Good night.'

'Good night.'

I closed the door, got behind the wheel and let it roll out of the yard, bumping the engine into life on the slope below. I drove slowly down the track and out onto the road. He could have been watching and didn't want him to see me driving fast. Once I was over the rise I put my foot down.

Up into the slope before crossing the brook and down to the flats and the bridge where two of us had been stranded a while ago in the snowfall and frost of early spring. The cars had been new ones that hadn't been fitted with cargo beds, and the cooling was such that the water froze while they ticked over and we were tinkering with the chains. They had been too long and we had gone down to Fornihvammur to shorten them, working in the lobby. It had been cold, wet work getting them fixed in place, then going for the heath road again with the cars so light and the wheels wouldn't grip.

I drove over the bridge and up the slope. It was steep and wasn't a road to take at any speed.

It was on these slopes that I had travelled a couple of hours in an old snow truck one April many years before. Back then we went elsewhere and didn't follow the road. We were proud of what the truck could do, but back then I was just sixteen years old with a hundred and sixty pound woman on my knee and paid no attention to the technical stuff they were so enthralled with as we drove blind through the snow that filled the still air.

I could go faster once the slope eased, and there were no more steep inclines until just before the refuge hut at the top of the heath. There wasn't much left in the bottle, so I took a swig and stowed it at my side on the seat. Just as I had expected, the wind was sharper as I breasted the long rise before the refuge hut. I could suddenly see down into Hrútafjörður and stopped the car to drain the bottle and throw it away. There was no wind on the water of the fjord and far out over the sea there were pink-striped clouds, with the sky to be seen behind them.

I lit a cigarette and set off downhill, as fast as the car would go and letting the engine run as fast as I dared past the Grunnavatn hills and the rough surface of the Holtavörður lake off to my left before it was soon behind me. Taking the slopes at a run, I had the car on my mind, and was still worried about it as I crossed the Hrútafjörður river and while I drove over the spit of land and took the fork up towards the stony banks.

It had been a poor winter, and the slopes had been deep in snow. Those on the scheduled routes drove big British army trucks over the heath. It was still hard going and the drivers had to keep getting out to stamp down the snow. Wrapped in our storm coats, we could see them through the frost-starred glass as they cleared snow away from under the wheels to stop them digging in. One of them out in the wind and the drifting snow watching to see how it was going as one truck inched forward. It was touch and go, and many of us were sick, puking over the exhaust pipe that lay all along the floor to provide some warmth for the passengers.

I drove up and out of Hrútafjörður, over the pass and the mountains of the Strands rose steeply, blue and distant from the sea, their peaks had been hidden by the low clouds. Coming out of Línakradalur I began to feel sleepy, with the dun hills of Víðidalur, the endless road and endless ridges still to come; sometimes passing hillocks, sometimes passes or bays. I could see the horses and some of them were close by the road. There were plenty of chestnut and brown horses, and I was getting very drowsy.

It was before we had fought. We went across to the canteen so that we wouldn't be drinking in front of the other drivers. The waitress brought us mixers and I topped them up from the bottle. She didn't think much of that.

'You're not allowed to drink in here,' she said.

'You're funny chick,' Guðmundur said. We were both pretty drunk.

'I'm saying you can't mix yourselves a drink here,' she said.

'Where are you from?' I said.

'From Húnavatnssýsla,' she said.

'That can't be right,' I said.

'And why not?'

'Because someone from Húnavatnsssýsla would never interfere with people having a drink.'

'I don't care. Those are the rules.'

'To hell with the rules,' Guðmundur said.

'I'll call the police,' she said.

'Do that and your ancestors will turn in their graves.'

'I won't hesitate if you're mixing drinks with booze here.'

'May you be trampled by thirty stallions.'

'That doesn't make any difference to the rules.'

'You're a good sort and you're from Húnavatnssýsla.'

'She can't be from Húnavatnssýsla, damn it,' Guðmundur said.

'You know as well as I do that you can't drink in here,' she said, so we went over to the parking lot.

The waitress was from somewhere up here, and she was a decent sort of girl.

By now I was very tired, wasn't noticing the countryside around me and before I knew it I was at Blönduós. The gauge showed there was plenty in the tank. I got out by the hotel and heard no sound but the cries of the gulls over the estuary and could feel morning in the air. After that we went past the bakery and I turned southwards along by the river. We crept across a shaky bridge and drove up to the hills, and we were getting along fine now after all those miles we had covered, and there was no more rattling that I could hear. I was fond of this car and it had served me well, as if it wanted our night-time journey across the country to be as smooth as it could be. It wasn't far now to reach home.

Langidalur was a just around the bend, then in towards Bólstaðarhlíð, over the high pass and we'd be there. I lit a cigarette and felt it smart as I put it in my mouth, and the fight was brought back into sharp focus. I don't remember why we had started to talk about Gógó. It was harmless enough to begin with, a question to ask if I had seen her recently… and then that I should stop seeing her…

'Why?'

'Because she goes around with Yanks.'

'And what business is that of yours?'

'She's a whore.'

I told him to shut his mouth but he wouldn't. He kept it up until I punched him. It was a miserable fight right from the start, seeing Guðmundur leaving and without being able to stand up and say that we shouldn't be angry with each other.

Leaving Langidalur, I took the bend. The Svartá river lay in loops down below and we were into morning. There was no arrival of morning as such, as the night had been bright. It wasn't a black-bellied night like in winter, when bright morning's arrival can't be missed, but more a change of the light from grey-white to a bright white. We took the slope at Bólstaðarhlíð at a run and followed by the turn into the Thverá valley, then uphill in second gear out of the turn, dropping down to first at the top of the slope and we did it like professionals. I gave the engine plenty of gas up to the pass, running fast past the marshes and we were at the peak just as morning broke properly. The lake below and the Blönduhlíð mountains and Hólmurinn and the ocean and the islands were all picked out in bright, clear colours and we pushed on down the slope.

There was a silver shimmer to the waves breaking on the water that brought a tear to the eye. Further down were the mountains over Sæmundarhlíð and there was a miasma of white water in the air over the Gýgjar falls. The hillsides were warming in the morning and I remembered that there were great northern divers on the lake on the low heath south of

106

Staðaröxl. We passed Arnarstapi and I could see on the stretch below that there had been some roadworks. I knew we were going fast and was about to slow down when everything was ripped out of my hands. I saw the road below me several times and tried to hold on tight. Then everything went dark.

Now the darkness has lifted and I can see it is still morning. There's no pain, but it's a strange feeling to be up in the air with my head on the edge of the road, looking out at Mælifellshnjúkur, Hamraheiði and Goðdalakista against the sky. More than likely I've been stunned by the crash and it's as well that I can't feel anything. I try to lift my head, but can't. So I can't see how things look up there on the road. The car must be badly damaged. Maybe I'm lying under it, but can't feel its weight. I can feel something warm run along my neck and into the hair at the back of my head. Now there's sunshine to the east on Mælifellshnjúkur. They say a white horse appears on the mountain when the winter snows loosen their grip in the spring. I can feel the damp and I don't like having to wait. There's definitely no white horse to be seen on the mountainside now. The damp continues to pool under my neck and there's nobody to be seen. It's still too early in the morning. Now it's getting dark and it's been wonderful to gaze on the mountains, just as it's going to be unpleasant waiting in the darkness. All the same, it's bearable, as I know the mountain is there and is waiting by my side.

11

They had been turning up at the rank since early in the morning and the first ones to clock in had been taking passengers on their way to catch buses, flights and ships. The call-outs over the loudspeaker had come thick and fast, and there weren't many of them in the waiting room at a time. Most of them were back between eleven and twelve and the parking lot was crowded as Guðmundur drove over the crossroads and into the street.

He parked by the kerb outside the canteen and it was a hot day with blazing sunshine as he walked out of the brightness outside and through the open door. He peered through his sunglasses at the men perched on their stools wearing checked shirts or light jackets, backs to him and shoes on the circular footrests. Leather pouches hung from their shoulders as they hunched over their plates. There were empty seats at the end. He walked along the rubber-matted floor and the line of backs, his head in the mirror passing along the line of faces.

He took a seat and the waitress asked what he wanted to eat.

There were men sitting all along the mirrored wall. These were healthy faces, as if the road was rooted deep in them, both the ugly side of it and everything that was beautiful. These were the old, mild-mannered faces of those who had seen much, the young faces of those waiting to know everything and the closed, indifferent faces. He ate quickly. Róbert watched him in the mirror. The large glasses hid his eyes, but not the puffed lower lip or the swollen jaw. Róbert knew that nobody had told him Ragnar had gone.

When Guðmundur had eaten, he crossed the road, threaded his way between the cars and to the rank's waiting room. He hung his number up on the rack. There were plenty of drivers ahead of him in the queue, so he took a newspaper and went outside to read, sitting on the wall next to the building. He was expecting Ragnar to appear at any moment and hoped that he wouldn't still be angry. It had been an idiotic fight. Róbert came over from the lunch bar, between the cars and over to where Guðmundur was sitting.

'Ragnar went up north,' Róbert said.

There were two men at the bottom end of the parking lot, dipping brooms into tubs of water and running them over the cars. The parking lot was very dry and clean after the rain.

'Ragnar went last night,' Róbert said.

Guðmundur seemed absorbed in reading and Róbert went back to the waiting room.

He heard the splashes of the pair washing cars, stopped reading the paper and stared at the rows of cars in the dry, clean lot under the mercilessly bright sun of the empty day. Later he went into the waiting room where there was nothing for him to do but wait to reach the front of the queue. It was hot in there, and some of them fussed over whether or not to turn the heating off. Fares were few and far between and there were too many cars outside. Guðmundur set up the chessmen and tried to solve a chess problem he had found in a newspaper on the table. The chessmen had not been used for a long time and the pieces were dusty and stained.

He had two fares before three in the afternoon and in between he did his best with the chess problem. After the second fare he went over to the canteen where the girl was pleasant to him. She had heard about the fight and had forgiven him his foul language. Back from the canteen, he wrestled with the chessmen.

The others had little to say to him and some of them expected to see Ragnar, that he would appear later. They played cards and stood staring out of the window, or sat on the benches as the air became increasingly stuffy. Occasionally a cloud would pass before the sun and some of them voiced the opinion that there would be rain before evening.

'A hundred and twelve. Laxargata ten,' the girl announced over the loudspeaker.

There was a while before a hundred and thirty-eight was called.

'It's quiet,' Eiríkur said.

'I'm going to pack it in,' Hæi said.

'We say we're going to quit and think about it seriously, but we never do,' Eiríkur said.

'I'm going to work at a petrol station,' Hæi said.

'Really?' Eiríkur said.

'My cousin's in the oil business,' Hæi said.

'I wish I had a cousin in some damned business,' Eiríkur said.

The card players were making plenty of noise and the brightness outside had faded as the sky clouded over completely.

'Sixty-eight, would you please come to the phone?' the girl said over the loudspeaker.

Guðmundur stood up. There were a king, a knight and a rook on the board and checkmate in three moves, but he could only do it in four. He walked past the reception desk. The girl was behind the glass, the receiver held to her face.

'Who's asking for me?' he said.

'There's a woman asking after Ragnar. She wants to speak to you considering Ragnar's not in town.'

'Who says Ragnar's out of town?'

'The guys,' the girl said.

'Tell the woman I'm not here.'

'I already said you were.'

'That's not my problem.'

'No, Guðmundur. Don't make me look a fool,' the girl said. She chewed flavoured gum, blowing bubbles, alternately deflating them or blowing them out.

'Put me through,' he said, heading for the call box. He knew it had to be Guðríður and lifted the receiver from its cradle. There was no window in the cubicle and they had never bothered to put in any decent ventilation.

'Hello?' he said.

'Is that Guðmundur?'

The woman's tone was composed, but he could feel that this was an act, that she had to be making an effort so that that impression would come across in her voice.

'Yes,' Guðmundur said.

'This is Guðríður Faxen. Good day to you.'

'Yes?'

'Do you know anything of Ragnar?'

'No.'

'I must see him.'

'That's no business of mine.'

'Aren't you his friend?'

'That's no business of yours.'

'Could you come and talk to me?'

'No.'

'I'll cover the fare.'

'There are a good few things you can't buy.'

'Don't bother. You can't offend me and I need to speak to you.'

'I'm not going to reply to this kind of hysteria.'

'If you're really his friend...'

'You don't need to remind me.'

'Then come and meet me.'

'What's so pressing that you can't talk about it on the phone?'

'It's better if you come.'

He hung the receiver back in its cradle and went out of the cubicle, through the waiting room and out into the parking lot. You can be a man's friend, go shooting with him, without expecting to undertake a task that should be a priest's. He swore, his words drowned out by the roar of the engine as he swept out of the parking lot. He drove along by the harbour, the same route as they had taken when Ragnar had taken the geese to her. It had been a generous and a pleasing thing to do. Back then it had been May and wonderful things happen in the springtime. The boy had been happy and there had been no reason to tell him about the weekends. On the other hand, it had hardly been possible to keep quiet, when everyone knew. Considering it had come to a crisis, it had been as well to tell him in person and cause him pain. Now it was July and he had been a happy man all that time, and for young men, life could be hard to bear.

Guðmundur stopped the car outside the shop. Through the window he could see people shopping inside. He got out of the car, went around the side of the house and through the door to the stairs leading to the floor above. She opened the door as soon as he rang the bell. He looked at the woman and could not understand why Ragnar had fought him. It didn't

113

matter if he was driving them or looking at them, once the carpet in the long hallway had been left behind you, along with the walnut and the pine and the paintings, they were only there for those who could afford them. They weren't there for youngsters who had nothing but the kindness of their own hearts.

She invited him in. He found it truly strange that she should ask after Ragnar.

'I don't know where to begin,' she said.

'There's nowhere to start. I told him that you're seeing Yanks at weekends. You have to bear in mind that lads like him take things to heart.'

The woman's eyes darkened and her face flushed.

'And you're his friends,' she said.

'The boys all knew and I didn't want them making fun of him because he loves you.'

'What boys?'

'The boys on the rank.'

'Neither you or these boys of yours can hurt him.'

'No. Listen to yourself.'

'When did you tell him this?'

'Late last night.'

She laughed and he could see how bitter she was, and it wasn't pleasant to listen to. It was uncomfortable to hear the triumph in her voice.

'He knew before you told him,' she said.

'What do you mean?' Guðmundur said, needing to sit down.

'I know because he was here earlier in the evening. I thought it had been him, so I called him. I remember he said it must have been some other car. And I said, no, Ragnar, it was you. He said, certainly not. I just came into town and went straight to the rank. But it was him.'

Guðmundur put a hand up to his glasses. He felt they had become very heavy and what he saw through them was dark.

'So why betray him?'

She didn't answer. She knew that this man could never understand her life, that she loved Ragnar and was now afraid that it was too late; that she had married too young and from that moment on everything had revolved around duty, lifeless and miserable, and nothing but money mattered; that she had searched for happiness among those who knew how to throw her a party; until she had realised that was empty worthlessness and that Ragnar's arrival meant they could start anew.

She had walked over to the window, her back to Guðmundur. She turned and went to him. She stood in front of him and gazed at the puffed lower lip and the bruised chin. She knew that Ragnar had done this; that he had fought for her.

'I want to go to him,' she said. 'You have to tell me where I can find him.'

'Ragnar went up north.'

'Where in the north?'

'I'll go with you,' Guðmundur said.

He hadn't expected this. They weren't like this, women like Guðríður Faxen. Suddenly she had become personable, standing in front of him in the gloom of his sunglasses, asking him for help to find the boy. In spite of everything, there were good days, good thoughts, good people.

'Can we go right away?' she said.

'We go early tomorrow morning,' Guðmundur said.

'Why not right now?'

'Tomorrow is better,' he said, thinking of his face and that it might be back to normal before they were to meet again.

It had started to rain as he stepped outside. His mood was lighter and he stopped off to get the car's oil changed. It was getting late in the day when he left the garage. He drove home, checked the tyres, and then went to the canteen for a bite to eat. The rain was coming down harder. The roads would be wet tomorrow.

From the canteen he went to the rank, where things were still quiet in spite of the rain. He hung up his number on the rack and sat on the bench to read the paper. Someone switched on the radio and a dance tune came from it, followed by announcements. Once the hour had struck, the news were read out and not a lot was happening in the rest of the world.

He heard the newsreader switch smoothly to national news '... fresh roadworks on a stretch of highway below Arnarstapi and the driver lost control of the vehicle on the loose surface. There were signs that the car had rolled several times. The car was on its side against the road and the driver had been thrown out and under the vehicle. His name was Ragnar Sigurðsson, a taxi driver from Reykjavík. He was pronounced deceased at the scene.'

There was silence in the waiting room. The newsreader continued with the news, until someone switched the radio off.

'A hundred and fourteen,' the girl's voice called over the loudspeaker.

Guðmundur still had the newspaper he had been reading in his hands. The others couldn't make out his eyes behind the dark glasses.

Akureyri
November 1954

Cab 79 and Iceland's transformation

Andy Lawrence examines the background to the film version of *Cab 79*, a landmark of modern Icelandic literature and cinema, with the film released as *The Girl Gogo.*

The film is better known than the book. It's remarkable that *Cab 79* (*79 af Stöðinni*) should not have appeared in translation before, considering just how much of a landmark Indriði G. Thorsteinsson's novel is in the eyes of Icelanders.

While it's a slim novel, it was also his first full-length work and when it appeared it was considered shocking. The book deals with the turbulence within Icelandic society as many of the old norms and conventions were being abandoned in the wake of Iceland's occupation by allied forces during the Second World War. First there were Tommies, and then GIs, bringing with them new demands, new luxury goods, and offering high rates of pay for local workers. Far from home, they were also interested in the local women – who were just as interested in these strangers with different manners and pockets full of cash.

Indriði G. Thorsteinsson's treatment of the subject is unadorned. It's a stark portrait of the post-War years as Reykjavík was being drawn inexorably into the modern age, only newly fully independent from the Danish crown and coming to terms with its new status - while still coping with the prejudices and hangovers of a previous era, including pre-War prohibition, the final remnants of which were only eventually repealed in the 1980s, as well as the controversial matter of the US military presence out at Keflavík at the far end of the Reykjanes peninsula south-west of Reykjavík.

The vibrancy of Reykjavík in *Cab 79* is juxtaposed sharply against the country's outlying areas where change happened slowly, and generally also reluctantly, with the book's protagonist torn between city life and his rural roots.

Indriði G. Thorsteinsson's book, written over the course of a few weeks at the end of 1954, shook up Icelandic literary life. One of Iceland's most successful contemporary authors, crime novelist Yrsa Sigurðardóttir, describes *Cab 79* as being Iceland's most important post-War novel.

Its style was something new, the sharp, unadorned delivery of the tale identified by reviewers at the time as being reminiscent of Hemingway. This was a writer who was just starting to flex his muscles. Not yet thirty, Indriði G. Thorsteinsson was a country boy from Skagafjörður in the north of Iceland – was is *Cab 79*'s protagonist Ragnar.

He hadn't come to this from a literary background, but instead had spent his younger years working on the roads, and again, like Ragnar, driving a truck and at the wheel of a taxi, much of which is reflected in the book. There's no mistaking his familiarity with the reality of being on the road, experienced before before finding his way to the city and into writing for a living.

Over a long career he produced half a dozen novels, collections of poetry and short stories, a number of biographies and non-fiction works and a a vast swathe of journalism, first as a reporter and subsequently with two long spells as the editor of newspaper *Tíminn.* There's no doubt that *Cab 79* was influential as well as popular. The first printing quickly sold out and it was rapidly re-printed to keep up with demand. The book influenced a generation of Iceland's writers in its willingness to take on controversial subject matter – and then came the film that was seen as just as controversial.

We've become accustomed to seeing images of Iceland's majestic landscape projected onto the screen at our local multiplex. The dramatic and varied landscape has made the nation a favoured filming location for blockbuster movies and watercooler TV series. In the last decade Iceland's lava fields, glaciers, deserts, and mountainous horizon have been captured on celluloid for *Captain America: Civil War*, *Interstellar, Noah, Prometheus*, and the *Star Wars* saga.

Alongside the relatively high number of visiting productions using Iceland's locations, screen talent, and technical facilities, the home-grown film industry has produced a number of internationally acclaimed movies since the establishment of the Icelandic Film Fund in 1978. The fund represented an important step in developing a self-sustaining film production culture. Previously, despite the presence of a domestic filmmaking community a lack of available funds and limited opportunities for exhibition restricted the number of Icelandic films produced. The early period of Icelandic cinema history included a notable documentary tradition and saw the release of several significant feature films including *Between Mountain and Shore* (1949), and *The Last Farm in the Valley* (1950).

Despite a filmmaking tradition stretching back to 1906, the industry went into an extended period of hibernation during the 1960s. As the world began to swing, new cinematic voices and ground breaking approaches to filmmaking emerged across the continent except in Iceland. In a decade that profoundly changed cinema the only feature films to be made in Iceland were *Hagbard and Signe* (1967), and a 1962 adaptation of Indriði G. Thorsteinsson's novella *79 af Stöðinni*, which was released internationally as *The Girl Gogo*.

In the age of Netflix and DVDs it is almost inconceivable that a third of a nation's population would go to see a film. 63,000 people flocked to see *The Girl Gogo*. This figure is even more remarkable when it becomes apparent that relatively few cinemas existed outside of Reykjavik which meant those eager to see the film attended screenings in village halls.

Demonstrating that Icelanders have a tradition of being keen to view adaptations of Indriði G. Thorsteinsson's novels, the 1980s film of his novel *Land and Sons* exceeded all expectations at the domestic box office and was seen by 110,000 people in a country with a total population of 230,000.

Positive reactions to *Land and Sons* proved that people were eager for homegrown content and would pay to see it. To cover production costs ticket prices were roughly 250% higher than competing international films. The inflated cost of admission did not deter cinemagoers who clearly had great enthusiasm for a domestically produced film that addressed national concerns.

Recognised today as the first sign that an Icelandic Film Spring was about to occur, *Land and Sons* can also lay claim to being the gateway to modern Icelandic film culture. In contrast, despite being one of two feature length motion pictures shot in Iceland during the 1960s the reputation of *The Girl Gogo* has dimmed in recent decades. Both films are faithful adaptations that retain the author's preoccupation with the loss of traditional Icelandic identity.

In part, *The Girl Gogo*'s slide into relative obscurity can be attributed to millennials' aversion to watching black and white films. Ironically, *Land and Sons* period setting doesn't appear to be as significant barrier for young generations of Icelandic cinephiles. Cineastes have been more keen to elevate *The Girl Gogo*'s place within the context of Icelandic film history. Among the contemporary auteurs paying homage to the film are Ragnar Bragason and Friðrik Thór Friðriksson. Readers may be surprised to learn that a film celebrated by two of the nation's most significant filmmakers isn't an Icelandic production.

With the national film industry in a state of suspended animation the only way for a celebrated novel to be adapted for the big screen was if a foreign production company bought the rights. Against all odds, that's what's happened. The presence of a Danish film crew on Icelandic soil may have rankled with those harbouring a grudge against their former colonial power and yet without foreign investment and an imported crew, 1960s Icelandic audiences would never had the opportunity to sit down in their local cinemas (or village halls) and see then relevant social and political concerns played out on the big screen.

For director Erik Balling *The Girl Gogo* may have been an opportunity to show audiences that he was capable of transcending the light comedic films for which he had become increasingly typecast. In his native homeland *The Girl Gogo* received a decidedly lukewarm critical response and the film is regarded as a minor footnote in a lengthy career. Today Balling's legacy largely rests on the television series *Matador*, a generously budgeted period drama that followed the lives of people in the fictional town of Korsbæk between 1929 and 1947. Against a backdrop of rivalries and class conflict, the series dramatised key moments of national history that were still within living history. It's tempting to consider that the series' central premise of a relatively self-contained community adjusting to changes in society was a return to themes previously explored by Balling in *The Girl Gogo*, albeit refracted through the prism of a costume drama.

Critical perspectives on the film have ranged from "scandalous" to "iconic". For non-Icelandic viewers unaware of the film's significance and the rich historical detail contained in each frame it's easy to dismiss *The Girl Gogo* as a fatalistic love affair. Careful analysis of Balling's film reveals a complex commentary on changes in Icelandic society as it grudgingly adjusted to the changes brought about by urbanisation, sexual politics, consumer capitalism, and the presence of American troops stationed at the NATO base in Keflavík.

The nation's relative isolationism came to an abrupt end in 1940 when British troops landed in Reykjavík harbour. In the wake of Denmark and Norway's occupation by German forces the British government feared that a Nazi invasion of Iceland would lead to the all-important North Atlantic shipping routes would be closed off to Allied forces. On the morning 10th May 1940 British troops boots pounded Reykjavik's streets and set in motion a chain of events that would permanently transform Iceland.

American troops replaced their British counterparts in 1941 and brought with them superior equipment, a relative abundance of spending money, new forms of music, hotdogs, hamburgers, and Coca-Cola. Icelandic dance bands incorporated British and

American hits into their repertoires. Performances by the state radio station's bandleader Bjarni Böðvarsson on air and in concert included Benny Goodman and Glenn Miller's most popular tracks. Previously, Icelandic bands performed traditional folk songs. The country was swinging to a new sound.

Having previously pledged to leave Iceland upon the cessation of conflict, the US government wished to maintain its military presence in Iceland. An approach to the Icelandic government to lease land near the small fishing village Keflavik for the purpose of establishing a permanent military base met with vociferous protests from irate citizens. A compromise was reached which allowed American troops to remain stationed in Iceland while troops were garrisoned in Germany. When the Icelandic government collapsed American forces withdrew from the country. Icelanders who feared the loss of national identity under the heavy weight of the American cultural blanket rejoiced.

US troops would return in 1951 and this time they'd bring television and Rock & Roll.

Iceland was one of the most significant beneficiaries of the Marshall Aid programme. Designed to kick-start the economy of a continent decimated by warfare and contain communist sentiment, Iceland's allocation was used to subsidise health and educations reforms, prop up ailing industries, and fund infrastructure developments. Having received forty million dollars, Iceland was obliged to repay a quarter. That Iceland qualified for the programme after having suffered comparatively mild damage, and yet received a large pay-out signified the American government recognised Iceland would play an important role in the post war era.

For a small nation the prospect of up to 50,000 troops being stationed at bases may have been interpreted by hostile citizens as being an invasion by stealth. During World War II American soldiers injected massive amounts of cash into the Icelandic economy and assisted with a programme of road, bridge, and building construction. Having gained independence from one colonial master, many Icelanders were aghast at the prospect of being subservient once again. Alongside continuing debates about the need to maintain independence, Icelanders were concerned that allowing American forces to return would erase any pretence at neutrality in the early days of the Cold War.

The 1960s was a transformative decade for Icelandic society. Icelanders had to adjust to the fact that American forces were apparently destined to stay. American influences seeped into Icelandic culture leading to fears that the indigenous language might be extinct within a generation. The tensions of this period have been dramatised in Thorsteinn's Jónsson's adaptation of Halldór Laxness' *The Atom Station* and Friðrik Thór Friðriksson's *Devil's Island*, based on Einar Kárason's novel. Both films examine Icelandic society in terms of modern history. They look at developments with reference to national identity and cultural imperialism.

Balling's *The Girl Gogo* was released while debates about the merits of NATO membership and American interventionism were raging in homes across the nation. Iceland's joining of NATO was highly controversial. Demonstrators gathered outside the Icelandic parliament and threw eggs and stones. When police attempted to disperse the protestors tensions escalated leading to a fight that forced the authorities to use tear gas to disperse the angry crowd. In the context of a decade which saw new waves determined to break with the old order and establish more radical and socially conscious form of cinema Balling was the quintessence of everything the nouvelle vague rejected. With *The Girl Gogo* he defied expectations and presented a film that was clearly indebted to the British Social Realist movement.

Shooting in real locations with Icelandic actors, the director took viewers on a tour of Iceland that had ceased to be a predominantly rural society. Two years prior to the film's release the number of people living in Reykjavik and its surrounding townships surpassed that of those inhabiting the countryside. The loss of rural traditions, and fragmenting of communities is a theme Indriði G. Thorsteinsson explores in *79 af Stöðinni* (*The Girl Gogo*) and *Land & Sons*.

The Girl Gogo begs the viewer to consider if taxi driver Ragnar (Gunnar Eyjólfsson) would have been happier and lived a more fulfilling life if he'd remained on the family farmstead. Perhaps Ragnar's fate was sealed the moment he decided to substitute a life of rural tradition for the prospect of easy cash driving a taxi selling smuggled bottles of alcohol to American servicemen. Ragnar poignantly falls in love with the tragic Gógó (Kristbjörg Kjeld). His masculinity is threatened after discovering Gógó's illicit liaisons with American soldiers. An everyman who has relocated to the city in hope of a better life, his dreams are torn asunder by unwelcome NATO troops. This doomed love affair played out the concerns of many Icelanders in the early 1960s.

In recent years *The Girl Gogo* has been introduced to a new generation in an unexpected way. Friðrik Thór Friðriksson, an avowed fan of the film, cast

Kristbjörg Kjeld as the lead in his 2010 movie *Mamma Gógó*. Submitted for the 2011 Oscars, the film saw Kjeld reunited with her former screen lover Gunnar Eyjólfsson in an exploration of how a family deals with their mother being lost to the ravages of Alzheimer's disease. Friðrik Thór Friðriksson's judicious use of scenes from *The Girl Gogo* celebrates both actors' achievements and is a fitting testament to the film's place in Icelandic screen history.

Andy Lawrence is a PhD candidate at Northumbria University. He is currently researching developing trends in Icelandic television drama production.

Made in the USA
Coppell, TX
29 July 2021

59672122R00080